NO WAY: TOTALLY TWISTED TALES

STORIES FROM PULPHOUSE FICTION MAGAZINE

Edited by
DEAN WESLEY SMITH

PUBLISHING

No Way:
Totally Twisted Tales

Published by WMG Publishing Inc.
Cover and interior design copyright © 2019 WMG Publishing Inc.
Cover art copyright © 2019 by dalarsen/Depositphotos
ISBN-13: 978-1-56146-083-0
ISBN-10: 1-56146-083-4

CONTENTS

INTRODUCTION

THE MOST TWISTED STORIES FROM PULPHOUSE FICTION
MAGAZINE

When I suggested this idea as a stretch goal for the *Pulphouse Fiction Magazine* Kickstarter subscription drive back in 2017, I had no idea how many really twisted stories I would be able to publish in the first year—plus Issue Zero.

Turns out it was a lot more than I can fit in this book.

In the first incarnation of this magazine, *Pulphouse: A Fiction Magazine* was known for publishing stories that wouldn't fit in any of the other magazines. And as an editor, that is sort of how my brain works.

And my own stories I write often go that way as well. Go figure.

So I suppose it shouldn't surprise me that a lot of really strange and twisted stories found their way into this second life of the magazine.

A few of the most twisted stories won't be here because readers and fans picked them for inclusion in the *You Really Liked That?* anthology and I have so many stories that would fit, I didn't want to duplicate stories between volumes.

Those stories are "Spud Wrangler" by Kent Patterson, "nanoturds" by Ray Vukcevich, "A Good Negro" by Ezekiel James Boston, and "In the Empire of Underpants" by Robert Jeschonek.

However, Kent Patterson, Ray Vukcevich, and Robert Jeshonek have different, equally twisted stories in this volume.

What do I mean by "twisted" for this volume? Simply put, high quality storytelling that often leaves a reader shaking their head in amazement that they read that story, let alone anyone wrote it.

Twisted stories often make you laugh, or make you tear up because they are always a surprise to the reader.

And twisted stories are often very memorable.

I would like to thank all of you who are reading this because you supported our first *Pulphouse Fiction Magazine* Kickstarter campaign. Your backing meant a great deal to all of us, including the authors.

The best way going foward to read all the really twisted stories in *Pulphouse Fiction Magazine* is subscribe and never miss an issue. Trust me, there will be many more coming up in the second year.

But for now, I hope you enjoy this sampling of some really fun stories. Really twisted stories.

Dean Wesley Smith
January 5th, 2019
Las Vegas, Nevada

THE WEREYAM

KENT PATTERSON

I published many of Kent Patterson's stories in the original Pulphouse Magazine *and it is again my pleasure to bring his strange and wonderful stories back to a new and modern audience.*

During Kent's short stint writing fiction before his untimely death, he had sold to F&SF, Analog, Pulphouse, *and many other magazines. I hope over the next few years to bring back most of those stories, if not all, for modern readers.*

This really twisted and very short story is one of Kent's "tuber tales," as he liked to call them. And yes, the title is accurate.

———

When the cloying odor of scorched marshmallow and hot yam filled the greenhouse, Bill Mauer cursed softly. Another damned premature. He got up from his watchman's cot.

The light of the full moon gleamed on the glass walls, throwing ghostly shadows over a jungle of yam vines as high as his head. He could see nothing, but the smell of hot candied yam grew stronger by the second.

Sighing, Bill picked up his auto-rooter. Nothing to do but find the premature and dig it out before the yam burst and let the bad strain of nanocritters contaminate the whole patch.

Bioengineered self-cooking yams had made his fortune. Self-cookers let even the busiest houseperson serve his/her family with nutritious meals with all of the rich goodness of genuine home cooking. But somehow the new, improved yams with the automatic self-candying option just weren't working out. He should have known better than to buy his yam nanotechnology from a firm calling itself "WerTech Transformations."

As Bill walked down the shadowy corridor sniffing out the premature, yam plants rustled in the wind, their dry leaves scratching against the glass walls. Now a yam runner caught around Bill's ankle, and he bent over to unwrap it.

Wait a minute. There's no wind *inside* the greenhouse. Spooked, Bill ripped the yam loose, but a dozen others gripped his other ankle. He kicked viciously, but more and more vines clutched at his arms and legs. He tried to scream, but a burning hot candied yam thrust through his lips, cramming itself into his mouth and choking off the air.

A sharp yam stem plunged into his jugular, and a hot wave of pain struck as tiny nanocritters surged through his arteries, multiplying in their millions, transforming every protein, every molecule of his body. His arms and legs withered away, and his torso grew large, globular, yam shaped.

And now Bill, for the first time in his life, understood yams. He understood the softness of the mothering soil. He understood sunshine, the feel of rain, gentle as butterflies' wings, upon yam leaves. But most of all, he understood yam pain, the brutal heat of an oven, the steel of a knife slashing through the skin.

Now he understood forks.

He understood cruel white teeth tearing at the tender yellow flesh, and all the degrading vocabulary of man's inhumanity to yams. Rage flowed through his body, white, screaming anger. He felt a thirst for vengeance which must be satisfied, and could only be satisfied with blood, enough blood to drown centuries of oppression, millennia of baked yams, boiled yams, yams on the side, yams with butter, yams with sour cream, and worse, yes, worse than all of those—candied yams.

Now the light of the full moon gleamed on the glass walls of the greenhouse. Bill's transformation was complete. Like a huge round moon he rolled to the greenhouse door, and a great rough beast, its hour come round at last, slouched towards the grocery stores to be born.

4

THE OLD GUY

ANNIE REED

Annie Reed's stories appear regularly in many varied professional markets and I am proud to say she is a regular in Fiction River.

Her story "The Color of Guilt" was selected for The Year's Best Crime and Mystery Stories 2016. *She is also one of the founding members of the innovative* Uncollected Anthology.

Since this is the fall issue, I thought this original story would be appropriate to have in here right before the holidays. And only Annie can tell a holiday story in a science fiction universe and give it heart.

———

Nick tried to get a job at a video store. He liked watching movies and knew quite a lot about classic gangster films, modern action-adventure flicks, and feel-good romantic comedies. He even liked the independent dramas that put everyone else to sleep. The store smelled like buttered popcorn, and large windows at the front and along the sides made the place feel light and airy. Nick thought a job like that might be a perfect fit for him.

The manager told him she wanted someone who could clean used movies at factory speed so the store could put them up for sale, and she asked if his eyesight was good enough to see scratches on the discs. He assured her that his glasses worked just fine and he had decades of experience meeting deadlines so he was sure he could work fast enough, but she said she thought he was better suited for something slower paced.

He applied for a position at a used bookstore. He'd always liked to read during his summers off. Fat fantasies and oversized thrillers, cozy mysteries and slim westerns, and romances that made his cheeks blush rosy red. He imagined days filled with the comforting smell of well-read paperbacks and the familiar task of sorting names in alphabetical order.

The pinch-faced bookstore manager spoke of a company philosophy based on continual criticism, and she gave him written tests with incomprehensible questions and illogical answers. For example, since when did a person's repeated inability to win a game mean the game was fixed? The manager assured him that was the right answer, but in Nick's experience, some people just didn't have an aptitude for games and there was nothing sinister about it.

The manager's thin face pinched even tighter when Nick shared his own philosophies about life and work and games with her. Even though Nick could calculate discounts in his head and recite the alphabet backwards, she thanked him politely and told him perhaps he should try placing a freelance ad as a life coach on Craigslist.

When Nick saw a Help Wanted sign at a self-service car wash, he stopped in to apply. He enjoyed being outside even when it rained or snowed, and the foamy, pink-tinged soap that bubbled up from long-handled scrub brushes reminded him of peppermint-flavored whipped cream. He assured the manager he knew how to make change and that he'd have no problem monitoring the equipment. The manager had him fill out a simple application, thanked Nick, and said he'd try to get back to him.

Nick never heard from the man again.

He thought about applying for executive positions with large, multinational corporations, but then he remembered the manager from the bookstore and the corporate philosophy her company had adopted from one of those large, multinational corporations. A job like that would steal his soul, bit by bit.

He applied for every position he thought he was remotely qualified for. As part of his job hunt, he took a number of increasingly bizarre online employment tests for which the internet assured him there were no right answers but which he seemed only capable of answering wrong given the lack of response to his applications.

He even applied at Walmart. They never called him back either.

It seemed like no one on the planet wanted a man with Nick's experience, his patience, his willingness to work, and most likely, his age. He thought about shaving his beard, or at least covering the bushy whiteness of it with a manly brown dye, but that felt too much like lying. Lying was a bad thing no matter how much psychobabble spin a person put on it. Nick wasn't a bad person. He just wasn't in high demand.

Well, no use crying over spilt milk, as his wife, God rest her soul, used to say. If no one on the planet wanted him, he'd just have to expand his search.

———

"You want to go to the moon?"

"Yes," Nick said with a smile.

The fresh-faced recruiter blinked at Nick across a conference room table made of glass and polished chrome. She was twenty-six, he knew, trim and professional in a dove-gray business suit, her dark hair pulled straight back from her high forehead. She wore a subtle perfume that smelled faintly of fresh-baked cookies and reminded Nick of hot chocolate stirred with a stick of cinnamon and topped off with a dash of nutmeg sprinkled on top of the miniature marshmallows.

The recruiter had been one of his kids in the days before his retirement from his previous line of work, and she'd always been good. Emily, her name was, although today she'd introduced herself as Ms. Wells.

She didn't remember him, of course. Nick didn't feel slighted. That was the way of the world, and he'd gotten used to it.

"How do you even know about the program?" she asked. "We're very discreet."

Nick expected the question. "A friend of a friend," he said, which wasn't a lie. Ms. Wells worked for Mr. Thrusher, who Nick knew as Alex, and Mr. Thrusher worked for a conglomerate owned by Mrs. Parker, the widow of Lincoln Parker, whom Nick had known as Linc.

Linc had dreamed of living on the moon when he was a little boy, and he had been a good little boy indeed. Nick had done what he could, giving Linc the kind of yearly gifts that encouraged him to look beyond the boundaries his well-meaning parents and teachers tried to place on his imagination.

Just because his kids eventually outgrew him didn't mean Nick lost track. He knew that Linc had grown into a man who took it upon himself to do the kind of things governments no longer seemed capable of doing. Today Nick sat in a conference room on the twenty-ninth floor of the tallest office building in Seattle, a building that owed its existence to the force of Lincoln Parker's dreams.

Mrs. Parker, whose name was Felicity, hadn't been a good little girl, but she'd grown into an honorable woman. Her husband had never given up his desire to go to the moon. Mrs. Parker intended to honor him by taking his ashes to the moon as a permanent part of the first colony established there—a moon base sponsored by no government or agency, affiliated with no religion or set of dogmatic beliefs, but spearheaded instead by Lincoln Parker's vast wealth.

Officially, the project didn't exist.

"You know, the program is the first of its kind," the recruiter said. "We expect conditions will be harsh. Perhaps you'd be better suited for..."

She let the thought trail off, as if she were embarrassed she'd made assumptions based on his white hair and beard and the round firmness of his belly.

Nick's smile grew wider. He was familiar with harsh conditions. He'd survived cold so deep it froze his breath and blizzards so fierce he needed help to navigate his way through the howling snow.

"I'd be right at home," he said.

She wasn't convinced, but she hadn't said no. Nick wondered if she didn't have the authority to say no—especially not to those people who'd discovered the program through a friend of a friend—and instead relied on gentle persuasion. Nick had been rejected by Walmart. He wasn't so easily dissuaded.

"This program is all about innovation," he said. "Be different. Innovative. Take a chance on the old guy."

Three weeks later, after a battery of physical tests and psychological evaluations that would have put the pinch-faced manager of the used bookstore to shame, that's exactly what Lincoln Parker's widow did.

————

Nick sat in a comfortable chair in a private jet headed toward Florida. He imagined it would be the last comfortable chair he'd sit in for quite some time.

A little patch of sunlight managed to make its way through the window next to Nick. The jet had lifted off from Seattle before dawn, and Nick had enjoyed watching the sun rise above the horizon as they headed east. Most of the flights in his life had been at night, and the warmth of the sun on his shoulder loosened his old bones. Although he'd still be able to see the sun from the moon, it wouldn't be the same.

Lincoln Parker's widow sat in a comfortable chair of her own across from Nick. Her second Bloody Mary of the flight sat on a corkboard coaster on the small cherrywood table between them. She hadn't touched much of it, even though she'd downed the first as soon as the flight had lifted off from the old Boeing field south of the city.

"I should have my head examined," Felicity Parker said to him.

Nick lifted an eyebrow, expressing curiosity without saying a word. He'd come to know Felicity Parker well during the last six months. She'd trained right alongside him while he'd learned the new skills he'd need on the moon. How to walk in an environment suit. How to walk at all in gravity lower than Earth's. How to interact with technology so advanced it seemed like magic.

He was somewhat familiar with that last bit, having used his own unique form of technology for most of his life to perform what seemed like magic to the rest of the world. He'd shown the skeptical youngsters in charge of getting him ready for life on the moon that it was possible, after all, to teach an old dog new tricks.

He'd been surprised that she intended to not only accompany her husband's ashes to the moon, but live the rest of her days there. She truly had grown into an honorable woman, one who was capable of deep, abiding love. Nick wondered if he'd misjudged her as a child. Good and bad were such subjective terms, after all.

When she didn't take him up on the invitation offered by his lifted brow, Nick shifted in his seat to look at her more directly. He'd rather look out the window, but they wouldn't arrive in Florida for another two hours. He still had plenty of time to take a last look at the places he had flown over so often in his life, even if he'd never seen most of them in daylight.

"You mean about your decision to participate in the program in your husband's place?" he asked. Going to the moon hadn't been her childhood dream.

She gave him a long look. She was a handsome woman of

forty-two with a strong jaw line and a direct gaze. A formidable woman in the boardroom, no doubt.

They were alone in the passenger area of the private jet. The other members of the team had left for Florida on a commercial jet the day before. Nick hadn't known why he'd been singled out to accompany Mrs. Parker, but it appeared she had something she wanted to say to him when no one else was around to hear.

"I remember you, you know," she said.

Nick's breath caught in his throat. He tried to cover his surprise with a quiet cough.

Even when they caught sight of him by accident, Nick's kids never remembered him, not after they grew up. After they quit believing. Only a rare few could recall his face at all. But Felicity hadn't been one of his kids, and she'd never believed.

"I was seven," she said. "And a precocious seven at that."

She had her hands folded neatly in her lap. She didn't glance away from his face like she was trying to remember the night. Her gaze was steady on his.

"I'd asked my mother for something foolish—a doll, maybe—but she told me I should write to you instead like all the other children."

She mentioned the doll in that offhand way adults sometimes did when they tried to camouflage the importance of what they were talking about. The doll had been something she'd wanted more than she was willing to admit.

She paused, clearly waiting for some response from him. Maybe she expected him to deny what she remembered, but really, what was the point?

"Did you?" Nick asked.

"It would have been a waste of time. Even if I'd believed in you, I knew I wasn't a good little girl. Oh, I wasn't particularly 'bad,' but I wasn't kind to my friends or my little sister." Now she did glance away. She studied her drink for a moment before she picked it up and took a quick sip. "I'm going to miss these, I imagine."

Alcohol wasn't part of the manifest for the first moon colony. The payload had been rigorously planned right down to the last piece of spare underwear. Everything they were taking with them was useful and necessary. Alcohol was a luxury, as was hot chocolate, apparently. Nick had had his last cup the night before.

Mrs. Parker held the drink, but she didn't take another sip. "I don't think my parents knew what to make of me. First child, odd child, so they doted on my sister instead. I'm sure the story is old to you, but when I was seven, my sister was the bane of my existence. She was the one who believed in you and the one you visited, but I'm the one who saw you."

Nick remembered Felicity Parker's sister. Monica. A cute little girl with golden ringlets and a sweet disposition. He'd brought her the toy she'd asked for. He hadn't brought Felicity anything at all.

Monica had died of leukemia when she'd been eleven. Nick had grieved for her, as he grieved for all his kids who left the world too early.

"Why did you allow me on the program?" Nick asked.

"I've asked myself that quite often, as a matter of fact." She looked at him again. "To deprive all the 'good' little boys and girls of your visits?" She sighed, an odd sound from such a self-assured, self-aware woman. "I'd like to think I'm not that petty."

"In case you're wondering, I'm no longer in that line of work," Nick said. "I've been…replaced. Downsized, I suppose you could say."

"And I could also say I was sorry to hear that, but I'm not sure that would be the truth."

Such an odd mixture of emotions. Nick wondered if every child who hadn't received a yearly gift from him would react the same way to seeing him after they'd grown up. Had that been part of the reason no one would hire him? What if it wasn't his age, but some long-forgotten and never quite forgiven slight that bubbled to the surface like an unscratchable itch just at the sight of him?

Felicity Parker straightened her shoulders and gave him a small smile. "Besides, now that I've gotten to know you, I don't believe you would have allowed yourself to be pushed aside if provisions hadn't been made for things to continue after you were gone."

She was right. There were still good little boys and girls in the world, and a system was in place to take care of all of them. It wasn't as personal a service as Nick had provided, but things changed as the world changed.

"Like your husband did," Nick said gently.

"Yes, like Lincoln did." She put the drink back on the corkboard coaster. "You asked me why I allowed you in the program. Why I overruled every one of my mission specialists who told me you were too old. Why I 'took a chance' on you, as I believe you told Ms. Wells."

She leaned forward, elbows on the table, her hands cradling her drink. The pilot made a slight course correction, and sunlight flowed from Nick's shoulder to his chest as the sun came more fully into view. The air in the cabin smelled stale like all recycled air did, but now he caught a whiff of her perfume and it masked the smell.

"I've always been a realist," she said. "I trusted what I saw with my eyes, what I experienced, that was what I knew to be true. When my sister passed away..." Her voice caught for just a moment, but her eyes remained clear, her gaze steady. "When she died, that was the end of my childhood. Then I met Lincoln. He was a dreamer, the opposite of me. He told me once that you encouraged him to follow his dreams, but he was never quite sure you were real. I knew you were."

And she'd never told him. As sure as he'd ever been about any of his kids, he knew that Felicity Parker had never told her husband that Nick was real.

"I don't believe in coincidences," she said. "I don't believe in fate. I believe in taking advantage of opportunities when they walk through my front door."

"I'm an opportunity?"

No one at any of the other places he'd applied had thought of him that way. They'd taken one look at him and dismissed him as useless.

"You encourage the dreamers," she said. "We wouldn't be here if you hadn't encouraged my husband. I expect that the people on this mission will need encouragement if we're to succeed."

All of that was more flattering than Nick had expected, but he wondered if he deserved it. Like Felicity, many of the people he'd be living with on the moon hadn't been among his good kids.

"Now it's my turn," she said. "I want to know why you applied for the program, and I don't want one of the pat answers you gave on the psych evaluations."

He'd written what he'd thought were the expected responses to any question that had even skirted around the edge of "why." Apparently his answers hadn't been as clever as he'd thought.

"I wasn't ready to be put out to pasture yet," he said. "Everywhere I went, no one else seemed inclined to give me a chance to prove I was still capable of anything beyond a quick game of checkers. What's that catch phrase everyone's so fond of? Think outside the box?" He shrugged. "Can't get much more outside the box than going to the moon."

He could see the disappointment in her eyes. He deserved it. She'd been more truthful with him than he had a right to expect, and he'd given her only a partial truth in return.

"This colony's going to make it," he said. "I don't know that for sure, but I can feel it in my bones. The people you've put together, they're exceptional at what they do. They say the technology's sound, and I trust that it is. People are going to do what people everywhere do, and the colony's going to grow."

Nick had seen the precursors of that. Some members of the team had already paired off. He wasn't the only one who'd noticed. The mission's payload included provisions for the children that would inevitably result.

"You might want me along to encourage the dreamers," Nick said, "but that's not my only job." He could feel the old twinkle in his eyes again, and saw the reflection of it in Felicity Parker's slow smile. "I guess I never did like the idea of being downsized."

———

Nick enjoyed the moon more than he thought he would. Lower gravity meant less pressure on his bones, and he felt like a young man when he got out of bed in the morning. That alone more than made up for the cramped quarters and the rough years when no one was sure the colony would last.

The colony had survived. More than that, it had grown as Nick knew it would. Over the years the colony had added a nursery and then a schoolroom. Felicity Parker tutored the colony's children in math and science, and Nick handled what colleges would have called "the humanities." They didn't criticize the kids but instead encouraged both logical and creative thinking, and celebrated their students' successes no matter how small.

"We're creating a society," Felicity Parker said to him one night over cups of instant hot chocolate.

Alcohol still hadn't made its way into the colony's food systems, but sheer demand had overcome the embargo on chocolate. Powdered hot chocolate wasn't as good as the kind Nick's wife used to make on top of the stove back on Earth, but after not having had any at all for years, the instant tasted like heaven.

"Better than the one we left behind?" Nick asked.

"I believe it is." She gave him a long look. "Are you ready for tonight?"

The colony had no trees to decorate, of course, and no chimneys to shimmy down, but those were minor details. Nick had adapted, just like he'd adapted to the recycled air and the need to wear an environment suit whenever he exited a building. What was important was the small satchel resting in the corner of his cramped room. The bag was stuffed to overflowing with gifts for the colony's children.

As she had every year, Felicity had overridden the safeguards that kept the colonists from creating frivolous things with the technology that made it possible for the colony to exist. With the safeguards off, Nick had created the kind of gifts for each of the kids that would encourage their dreams—dreams he'd learned about by listening to them as he taught.

He finished off his hot chocolate before he lifted the satchel. Felicity Parker had become a good friend. Her help in assisting him with the reversal of his downsizing was invaluable. The biggest change Nick had made in how he did things this time around was due to her.

Nick no longer kept lists of who was good and who was bad. "Good" and "bad" were no less harmful labels than "old" and "slow" and "useless." Kids were kids, and every kid deserved to know someone believed in them.

Just like Felicity Parker had believed in him.

Nick winked at her as he left his room and enjoyed the quizzical look she gave him in return. No matter. She'd find out what the wink was all about soon enough.

This year he'd created an additional gift and tucked it beneath the other gifts at the bottom of his satchel so she wouldn't accidentally catch sight of it. He'd leave the gift at her door after he'd delivered all the rest. It was a totally frivolous gift, something that she'd wanted when she was seven but didn't believe she deserved.

It was long overdue.

PLAYING WITH TRAINS

J. STEVEN YORK

J. Steven York has a name for this group of stories he writes that I am not going to repeat due to the political climate we live in. Let's just say that Steve has the ability to take a trend in society and twist it to a logical but horrifying conclusion.

This is one of those stories.

And he often does the same thing in the wonderful internet comic we are running every issue on the last page.

———

David Drummond sank back ino the soft leather upholstery and smiled across the limousine at his uncomfortable passenger. It was a good day to be rich and ruthless.

He watched as Prescott inserted a pudgy index finger under his collar and tugged nervously. Despite the air conditioning, sweat beaded on his brow. Still, there was an air of impending triumph on the man's face. That didn't concern David in the least. "You seemed surprised, Mr. Prescott, when I offered you a ride to the train station."

Prescott squirmed, and pulled his shoddy vinyl briefcase close to his chest like a shield. "You know that I didn't bring any good news to your father. Fast Path Systems is only a little company compared to Drummond Dynamics, but I and the rest of the board are determined to pursue our patent suits against you to the very end. Our case is solid. We will win."

David looked over his shoulder as Trenton, the butler, climbed in behind the wheel. "The bags are in the trunk, Master Drummond."

"To the station then." He winked at Trenton. "You know the way." He turned back to Prescott. "You were saying?"

"I was surprised at your hospitality, yes. In fact, I was—" He laughed nervously. "—I was almost surprised to get out of there at all. There are stories—"

"—of people who have crossed the Drummonds disappearing mysteriously," David completed the thought. "All true, I assure you. I've killed many of them myself."

Prescott's eyes bugged, and his face went white and translucent as a cake of ice. He began to slowly sink down behind his briefcase.

David waved his hand to calm the man. "My father's interests in this are not necessarily my interests. I'm going to help Fast Path systems. I'm sure you don't know it, as I've taken great pains to conceal the fact, but I'm a large stockholder in your company. Your promising patent suit has caused the stock to soar, and it would be to my advantage for that to continue for a while."

Prescott uncoiled like a watch-spring. "You said you'd help us?"

"Help Fast Path? Certainly." David leaned back and watched the countryside roll by. "For instance, I'm going to tell you that, while you were in the mansion, your briefcase was replaced by an exact duplicate. Identical but for one detail: a bomb concealed in the lining."

Prescott jumped and emitted a little squeak, but to his credit he didn't drop the briefcase.

"It's quite safe. Father had planned to set it off by remote control when you met with the rest of the Fast Path board of directors. Some plan of blaming it on terrorists, I think, and of taking advantage of the confusion and resulting stock plunge to cheaply acquire Fast Path."

Prescott seemed uncertain. "Why should I trust you? Why would you help us against your own father? Your own company?"

"I don't own a bit of Drummond Dynamics, or any other Drummond company. Maybe I will someday, if I meet my father's expectations, but not now. I have a little money my mother left me, which is how I got the Fast Path stock, but that's it. Prescott, my father treats me like a child. I'm twenty-two years old, and capable of looking after my own interests." He looked at Prescott. The businessman was relaxing again, though David noticed that he'd pushed the briefcase to the far side of the seat.

"Do you know," continued David, "what he got me for Christmas this year? A train set. Can you imagine, giving a grown man such a thing? A train set!" He snorted with disgust. "I can take care of myself, and I'm going to demonstrate that to Father."

They pulled into the parking lot of the little country station, a red building with lots of Victorian gingerbread. A diesel horn could be heard in the distance.

"Right on time," said David.

Prescott hesitated. "This isn't the station where I arrived."

"I took the liberty of having Trenton change your arrangements. This station is no farther than the other, and we wouldn't want father to find out about this discussion, would we?"

The idea seemed to frighten Prescott. "No, we certainly wouldn't."

They hurried up to the small covered platform, Trenton struggling along behind with the bags. The offending briefcase stayed in the car.

Prescott watched the approaching train. "I can't thank you enough, Mr. Drummond. We're going to bring your father down. Even if I can't make attempted murder charges stick, we're going to win this suit, and your profit will be phenomenal."

"You misunderstand me, Prescott. I'm thinking in the short term. Nobody wins against my father. When this plot fails, there'll be another, and another, until ultimately Fast Path will fall. I've bought Fast Path to hold for a month or two at most, during which time I'll make a nice profit. Then I'll sell out just before the inevitable end. I still stand to inherit the Drummond companies, and I wouldn't do anything to hurt them in the long run. We'll see what happens with your other charges, but I'm not worried."

Prescott's face wrinkled like he'd bitten into a bad grape. "You disgust me." He turned his back on David to watch the train pulling into the station. "You Drummonds are all alike."

David laughed quietly. "We are, in a way, Mr. Prescott. You see, you know far too much." He lifted his foot and kicked it hard against the small of Prescott's back, sending the man flailing off the platform.

Prescott almost had time to scream before the train rolled over him.

David laughed, and looked up into the blind, plastic eyes of the engineer, perpetually leaning from the locomotive's cab. He carefully pulled a radio control box from his pocket and turned a knob. The rumble of the locomotive's engine changed, and the brakes squeaked as passenger car after empty passenger car clicked past, and the train slowly rolled to a stop just beyond the station.

David walked to the edge of the platform and looked down at the tracks. It smelled of diesel fumes and fresh blood. "Trenton, clean up this mess. And call my broker. Tell him to sell Fast Path at eighty-seven and use the profits to order a new caboose and a half-dozen assorted freight cars." He shook his head in disgust. "A train set, father? Well, I'll show you that I can buy my own toys."

HAND FAST

KRISTINE KATHRYN RUSCH

Over thirty years ago, Kristine Kathryn Rusch and I started Pulphouse Publishing. Kris did the editing, I did the publishing stuff, and Pulphouse grew quickly into the fifth largest publisher of science fiction, fantasy, and horror.

Kris not only was the executive editor of all of the Pulphouse lines of books, but she edited the award-winning Pulphouse Hardback Magazine *for its twelve volume planned run. Then she stayed on as book editor, but her short fiction editing took her to* The Magazine of Fantasy and Science Fiction, *where she stayed as the only woman editor for six years. She is the only person in history to win a Hugo Award for both her editing and her writing.*

With her going to F&SF, we decided I would edit this magazine, keep the high quality fiction, just put it in a different format. She stayed at F&SF from 1990 until 1996 and I edited the first incarnation of this magazine from 1991 until 1996. To say our house was full of manuscripts and stories in those years would be an understatement, since we both got over a thousand per month, in large envelopes. (shudder)

Since then, she has written hundreds of novels and even more short stories and won just about every award that is offered in the different genres of fiction. I talked her into letting me publish this story here and I have a hunch you are going to love this story as much as I do.

The most romantic gift anyone ever gave me? A gun.

Valentine's Day, ten years ago. Ryder. God, what a sweet man. Six-three, all tattooed muscle, black hair shorn off that year to accent his dark, dark skin.

We were on the roof of his place, trying to keep candles lit in the cold breeze blowing across the Hudson, eating take-out sushi with custom-made chopsticks clutched in our frozen fingers, sitting on lawn chairs wedged into the ice-covered snow.

Ry gave up on the candles midway through, decided to go to

his apartment to get a lantern—he said—and did come back with one. Battery operated, large, already on. And in his other hand, a Tiffany's blue box big enough for a cake, tied with the ubiquitous white ribbon.

Despite the box, he couldn't afford Tiffany's. Not even something small, and certainly not something that large. Even if we could have afforded Tiffany's, we wouldn't have bought anything there.

We were militantly anti-ostentation back then. It went well with our lack of funds. But we *believed* it, acted on it, maybe even looked the other way when someone in a silk suit and shiny leather shoes ventured into the wrong alley, stepping in only when that rich bastard looked to be in trouble for his life—never stepping in to save his wallet.

I opened the box with trembling fingers, stuck the ribbon in my pocket and stared at a small lockbox that looked old and well used.

Ry nodded. He wanted me to open it.

So I did.

And saw the gun.

It wasn't any old gun.

It was custom-made, silver, and, I later learned, it glowed slightly when its owner touched it. It also designed its own bullets—silver for werewolves, holy-water-laced for vampires, and laser-lighty (filled with fire) for the unknown magical.

I long suspected—and never tested—that the miracle weapon could transform its bullets into whatever the owner imagined.

We handfasted me to the weapon. He claimed he had another one, but I never saw it.

Handfasting required the candlewax (he was planning ahead), a bit of mercury, a touch of burnt almond. And some other magical oil-based concoctions I'm not going to describe, just in case.

And yeah, handfasting—pagan term for wedding. But it also meant a bargain struck by joining hands. I thought then that applying hand to hand-grip was the same thing.

I had no idea where Ry had gotten the weapon or how he learned to control it. I didn't understand why he gave it to me.

I'd love to believe what he told me that night: He gave me the gun because he loved me.

But that couldn't have been entirely true, because who gave a gun out of love?

When I pushed the next day, asking the right way—*what made you think of me when you saw this?*—he said I was so much more talented than he was, I deserved the weapon, and the weapon deserved me. And then, the day after that, he admitted he had one too, and we'd go practice with them, just him and me, Upstate, the next time we had the dough.

There was no next time. There wasn't even a day after that. Not for Ry.

Someone caught him in our alley, shredded him, took the tattoos as souvenirs. I found him, still alive, barely. But not alive enough to tell me what happened. Or alive enough to let me know he heard me when, stupid me, I told him I loved him for the first and only time.

———

Fast-forward a decade to the winter that never died. Press coverage that year pegged it as the coldest in two decades, blaming arctic air that should've lived in Canada but, like any other snowbird, decided to move south.

I had my own place by then, two buildings over, tall enough to get the occasional sunset glinting off the nearby roofs. I liked that: the dying sunlight reached the kitchen of my glorious apartment, just about the time (in the winter at least) I was having whatever it was I scrounged for breakfast.

My apartment: three rooms, hard-fought. Actually purchased when the building went condo just before the damn housing crisis. Now I was—as the pundits so euphemistically call it— underwater, and for once, I gave a damn.

Then I'd come to my place, warded and spelled, with the most comfortable furniture I could find (mostly discards on garbage day, dragged up the elevator, refurbished and softened), and reveled in having a safe harbor, somewhere no one else ever breached. Not anyone, including the post-Ry lovers, the so-called friends, the clients and the hangers-on.

Just me and the silence I'd created, a place to refurbish myself after each day's hard knocks and scrapes.

Somehow I stopped being militantly anti-ostentation. I was still anti-ostentation—no one would mistake the interior of this place for anything fancy—but I'd grown up enough to have financial entanglements and to adopt some of the trappings of a good citizen.

Protective coloration, really.

I'd needed it.

Back in the day, me and Ry were a team, and he was the stronger. We'd partner up, go after the shadows, fight till dawn, screw till noon, sleep a little, and start over.

Then he died, and I went full-moon batshit crazy searching for his killers, never sleeping, the edges of the world growing jagged and dark, finding clues where none existed, missing clues that'd probably been there, going, going, going until I ended up face-down in an abandoned subway tunnel and no memory of how I got there.

I had to choose, with my face pressed against the oil and the decades-old piss, whether I'd keep going or whether I'd just let it all end.

And weirdly, it was Ry who saved me. Ry, with his crooked half-smile and his embrace of anything dangerous. Ry, who had a tattoo on his left bicep of a bright yellow smiley face holding a sword in one little gloved hand and a dripping scalp in the other, with the word *Onward* in gothic letters underneath.

That tattoo always made me grin, especially when he flexed it, making the sword move up and down as if the smiley face were marching at a parade.

I saw that tattoo as clearly as if it were in front of me and, instead of regretting the method of its theft, I let out a tiny laugh. That moved the dusty dirt in front of me, and almost made me gag on the stench. Which, for some reason, I also found funny.

I was exhausted and spent, and in some ways, ruined. Completely different than I had been before.

I sat up, then stood up, and staggered my way out of the tunnel, heading back into my life. Which I rebuilt—alone—bit by bit. In the places that had never functioned alone, I built—I trained, I learned, I *became*.

I stayed in the City. Because the City had taken Ry from me. I couldn't get him back: Magic didn't work that way—at least not any kind of magic I chose to participate in. But I could find the missing pieces.

I could find whoever or whatever had killed him.

I could have answers—

Or so I thought. At first. Before I realized that a girl's gotta eat. A girl's gotta live. A girl's gotta move forward.

So I did.

———

And then the winter of our discontent. Valentine's Day wasn't a bright spot for anyone. Yet another storm had arrived the day before, canceling flights, snarling traffic, and delaying the all-important flower deliveries to shops that relied on them. By the time the actual holiday rolled around, the City was enveloped in sleet on top of two feet of snow.

I rented an office near the alley where Ry got attacked. The office wasn't much—third-floor walk-up with a frosted door, frosted windows, and a radiator that clanged to its own tune but at least kept the place warm. I had an actual desk which I got from an office five doors down—a blond wood monstrosity that smelled like old cigarettes, giving the office a slightly musty air, something I actually liked. In keeping with the thirties motif, I kept an open bottle of Scotch in the bottom drawer, although I rarely touched liquor. Any more.

I cribbed an old leather sofa from that same abandoned office, and found two matching desk chairs in the garbage behind my apartment building. The only money I actually spent on furnishing the place was for my chair, which was the most high-tech thing I owned. It had more levers and dials and options than the first (and last) car I ever drove.

The office had no computer or phone or anything remotely resembling office equipment. I don't write reports. I collect funds up front, and don't give paper receipts. If I need more money from my clients, I ask them for more. If they refuse to pay, I refuse to work.

I'm not one of those private detectives who works *pro bono* because the case interests them. I work because I need the money —and if I didn't work, I'd go back down that crazy subway tunnel, and the overwhelming stench of decades-old piss.

It's not even fair to call me a private detective. I use the title sometimes because it's easier than explaining what I do. What Ry and I used to do. What I never stopped doing, after he was gone.

I shove the magic back where it belongs.

Sounds easy, but it's not. And there are only a few of us that can do it.

By now it should be clear: I wasn't sitting alone in my office on Valentine's Day because of the snow. I hated Valentine's Day with a bloody passion. I tried not to. It wasn't the fake holiday's fault I was always so miserable at this time of year.

I usually tried to tell myself that Valentine's Day had peaked for me that night on the roof, with the lantern and the Tiffany box. And sometimes that worked.

But not on the tenth anniversary. Not as I slogged my way through the snow and sleet, watching inane couples in their finery get out of cabs or stumble out of the subway, pretending the day (night) was perfect after all. Maybe it was the combination—wind, snow, Valentines—that caught me.

Or maybe I was finally feeling my age for the first time.

Whatever it was, it convinced me to haul out that open bottle of Scotch the moment I collapsed into my high-tech desk chair. I had had the same open bottle of Scotch for months now, ever since a baby demon with a heart of gold (long story) had slept in my office for two weeks and nursed on the bottle like it was demon-mama's teat. No way was I ever drinking from that bottle again. So I got a new one—after I found baby demon's distraught mama and finally reunited the two of them.

Me, an open bottle of Scotch, sleet tapping the frosted glass like werewolf claws. I thought I had the night all planned—when the gun appeared out of nowhere.

The gun. You know, the one from the Tiffany's box.

Or so I thought at first.

Well, not entirely true, because you don't think about where a gun came from when it appears right in front of you, business end pointed at your face, trembling as if held by an unsteady hand.

And nothing else.

I set the bottle of Scotch down, then made myself calmly and deliberately screw the cap back on. I would have put the bottle back in the bottom drawer, but the gun's trembling got worse, and I really didn't want to get shot just because I was being a neat freak.

I wondered what kind of bullets were in that thing—silver, holy-water-dipped, flaming hot. Damn near any of them would kill me, since I'm just good old-fashioned flesh and blood. I stared at the wobbling muzzle of that gun, then realized I had some control.

We'd been handfasted after all. The weapon belonged to me and I to it, which was probably why it couldn't go through with the shooting.

I held up my right hand and said in my deepest, most powerful voice, *Come to me.*

The weapon's trembling increased, but it didn't move. My heart moved enough for both of us, trying to pound its way out of my chest.

I tried the command again, and again, the damn gun just shook more.

So, figuring the rule of three, I tried one final time. *Join your handfast partner.*

The gun stopped trembling. And then it whirled as if pursued, and floated away from me. I sat for a moment, stupidly, then realized that the damn gun didn't belong to me. It was a different weapon than the one locked in the lockbox I kept in the Tiffany's box.

I got up and stumbled after the gun. It floated down the hall-way, then down the stairs, always staying at chest-height, just as if someone were holding it.

It reached the lobby, bumped out the door (I have no idea how it got open), and into the sleet. I followed, coatless, instantly chilled, and nearly slammed into a couple wearing fewer clothes than I was, giggling their drunk way out of a nearby bar. They didn't seem to see the gun, but I couldn't take my gaze off it.

Because it went into the alley, where Ry died. And then it started banging against the brick wall behind a Dumpster, as if it were trying to get into something.

I wished for gloves. And boots. And a coat. I was sliding on ice, and still the alley had the stench of weeks-old garbage. It didn't matter how cold or wet something got, the smells remained.

I tried not to look at the back corner, where Ry bled out. It was covered in a snow pile six feet high anyway. The gun kept banging and scraping, and I finally decided to violate one of the major rules of automated magic.

I got between the gun and the wall. The gun kept hitting the same brick, scraping it white. I grabbed the damn thing, surprised that my fingers fit where the mortar should have been.

So I pulled.

The brick slid out easily, and I slid backwards, nearly falling. I caught myself on the edge of the ice-cold Dumpster.

The gun turned itself sideways, shoving its grip into the open hole. It had stopped trembling.

It balanced on the edge of the brick below for just a moment, then toppled downward.

I jumped back, afraid it would go off by accident.

But it didn't.

It rested on top of the ice as if all the magic had leached out of it. Its color was different too. No longer silver, but a muddy brown instead. I tilted my head, blinked hard, my face wet with sleet.

I wiped my eyes with the back of my hand, smearing the cold rather than getting rid of it.

The gun still looked odd. I figured it actually looked odd—it wasn't my magical sight that had changed; the gun was different.

So I crouched. And looked closer.

And gasped.

Something had wrapped itself around the grip. Brown and mottled. It took a moment for my eyes to make sense of what I saw.

The word *Onward* in Gothic script.

Bile rose in my throat.

I nudged the gun with my foot, then managed to flip the weapon over. The image on this side was a distorted yellow, desiccated and faded.

I swallowed hard, my stomach churning.

Then I stood and made a small flare out of my right fingertip. I used the flare to illuminate the hole in the bricks.

Saw shreds, images. Messed on the top like someone had rifled a drawer, and laid flat below, like carefully folded linen napkins waiting for a fancy dinner.

I lost my not-fancy dinner. And breakfast. And every meal for the past week.

Some investigator.

I'd searched for those patches of skin from the very beginning —all six of Ry's tattoos—knowing his magic lurked in them.

Only, as I braced one hand on the wall, and used the other hand to wipe my mouth, I realized that there were a lot more than six scraps of skin in that wall.

A lot more.

I allowed myself to get sick one final time before hauling out my phone, and calling the only detective at the NYPD who would ever listen to me.

Ryder's older brother.

Dane.

––––––

He showed up ten minutes later, wearing a dress coat over an ill-fitting suit, and a this-better-be-worthwhile attitude. He wore his hair regulation cut, and he didn't have the muscles or the tattoos. Still, there was enough of a family resemblance to give me a start every time I saw him walk toward me. Same height, same build, same general energy.

"Three-hundred dollars up front for dinner," he said. "Includes five courses and champagne. We'd just finished appetizers."

"Special girl?" I asked.

"I'm hoping," he said. "We'll see if she's still there when I get back."

She might be waiting a long time, I thought but didn't say. I just showed him the open hole in the brick.

"What?" he asked impatiently.

"Just look," I said, my voice raspy, throat sore, my breath so foul I tried not to face him.

He grabbed his phone and used it like a flashlight, then backed away when he realized what he was looking at.

"What the hell?" he asked.

He peered into that obscene storage space, then looked at me, his handsome face half in shadow.

"How did you find this?" he asked, as if I had created the horror all on my own.

I poked the toe of my battered Nike against the gun.

He turned the phone's light toward it, saw the desiccated but still visible smiley face, and swallowed hard, then shook his head.

"You're out here without a coat or hat or mittens, and you're telling me you just stumbled on this gun?"

He didn't mention his brother's skin, wrapped around it, or the fact that there was more shredded skin in that opening.

"No, I'm not saying that."

Now that he mentioned how I was dressed, I realized just how cold I was. My teeth started chattering. I shoved my hands in the pocket of my jeans, not that it did much good.

"I asked you how you found this?" Dane snapped.

"And I showed you," I said.

"It means nothing." His voice went up, echoing between the buildings.

"Only because there are some things you refuse to let me tell you," I said, matching his tone.

He stared at me, breathing hard. I tried to stay calm, but it was difficult, considering how bad I was shivering.

"Magic?" he asked with a sneer he once reserved for Ry, but had transferred to me since Ry's death.

I nodded.

Dane rolled his eyes and shook his head. "You think this crap has been here all along?"

I shrugged one shoulder.

"You want to tell me, without talking about magic, how you came down here?"

I sighed. I could have said no, I supposed, but I didn't. "I followed the gun."

"And whoever was holding it," he said.

"I didn't see who was holding it," I said.

"Convenient," he said, "since it looks like Ry's gun."

It is Ry's gun, I wanted to say, but knew better. Because then Dane would ask me how I knew that, and I would point to the layer of skin wrapped around the grip.

"Ry told me he had one," I said. "I never saw it. How do you know it's his?"

Besides the skin, I mean, I added mentally. Of course, Dane didn't hear that.

"Pretty unusual thing, huh?" Dane said. "Ry called it magic. Me, I think it's some kind of toy, since it supposedly invents its own bullets."

I ignored that jibe. "He ever use it in front of you?"

"No, he wanted to take me to the range to practice with it, but he…." Dane let out a sigh. "He died before we could go."

"Who ended up with the gun?" I asked.

"I don't know," Dane said. "I never saw it again."

"So you remember it after *ten* years?" Lying on the ice, with Ry's skin wrapped around it, the gun didn't look *that* distinctive, at least not to me.

"I'd tell you I recognized it by that lovely silver barrel," Dane said, "but I didn't even notice that part at first."

I waited. I was going to make him say it, the bastard.

"I don't think we're going to have to test the DNA on that skin," Dane said quietly.

I nodded.

"But we might have to on the rest of this stuff in here." Dane peered at that hole. "Why would the gun turn up now?"

It had been exactly ten years since I got my gun. But I had no idea if Dane knew I had one too, and I wasn't about to tell him.

"The anniversary's coming up," I said.

"Yeah, like I can forget that," Dane said dryly. He sighed again. "I'm going to call this in. You need to go inside before you freeze solid."

"What about the gun?" I asked. "Do you think it should go into evidence?"

He looked at me. He knew what I was thinking. Hell, all of New York would have known what I was thinking. The City had seen a lot of news lately about weapons stolen out of the NYPD's evidence storage.

"You want to pick it up?" he asked.

Of course I didn't. Neither did he. But he had opened the door, and he was the magic-denier, not me. I reached around him, and with shaking fingers, sorted through the Dumpster until I found a box that wasn't too junked up. It was a shoebox with some stains along the bottom, but it didn't smell that bad, so I grabbed it.

I was going to scoop up the gun with the box lid, but I stopped halfway. I didn't want to mess up that grip. (That tattoo.) So I glanced at Dane. He was watching me closely.

I slid the lid underneath the box, then held the box in my left hand. I turned my right palm upward. Then I concentrated on the gun and hooked it mentally to my right hand. Slowly I raised my hand, and the gun rose too.

Once the gun was a foot off the ground, I crouched, slid the box underneath it, and turned my palm down. The gun bounced into the box, and I slapped the lid on it.

Dane watched me, face gray in the half light. His gaze met mine, but he didn't say anything. I knew, if asked, he would say only that I slid the box under the gun and scooped it up.

I offered him the box.

He shook his head. "You keep it."

"There could be evidence here," I said, taunting him.

He shook his head. "We'll have more than enough. Now, go inside."

He didn't have to tell me twice. I scurried to my building, feeling as if I would never get warm again.

———

So Ry had handfasted to the gun, just like I had.

I carried it up the stairs to my office, noting that the box did have an odor, but I wasn't sure if the odor came from the Dumpster or that tattooed slice of skin. I didn't want to think about that either.

Instead, I locked the entire box inside my office safe. Then I went to the ladies room down the hall ostensibly to run warm water on my hands but, in reality, to get whatever was on that box off my skin.

I shivered and shivered, even after I warmed up. The shivering didn't just come from the cold.

After I'd cleaned up, I grabbed my heavy down coat, my unattractive knit cap, and my gloves. I slipped everything on, locked the office, and headed home.

I needed to know if my own gun was still there.

When I reached the street, the cold returned with a vengeance. It was as if I hadn't gone inside to get warm at all.

A crime scene unit had the alley blocked off. Dane appeared to have left, and some unis guarded it all. They stared at me as if I were the bad guy. I pivoted, went the other way, and headed to my place.

At least the sleet had stopped, but the sidewalk was slippery. The restaurants along the way—this place was so gentrified now —were filled with well-dressed couples pretending to be happy. And maybe they were over their—what had Dane said? $300 meals? I preferred the take-out sushi eaten with custom-made chopsticks on a roof so cold it made this evening seem like the Bahamas in summer.

I still missed Ry, the bastard. I liked to think I had moved on, but I hadn't. Not inside. Not where it counted.

I took an elevator to my apartment, and let myself in. The apartment was warm, homey, perfect, just like it had been since I bought it. I closed the door and locked it, then checked the wards just in case.

They were fine.

I peeled off my gloves and tossed them on an occasional table. Then I went into my bedroom and opened the closet.

There, on the top shelf, was the Tiffany's box. I pulled it down, and gingerly untied the ribbon. I tugged the lid off and looked inside. The lockbox was still there. I opened it too, and stared at the gun, gleaming in the light.

It looked no different than it had every other time I had looked at it. It was a shame I had never used it, a shame that it hid here in the dark, as if it were at fault for Ry's death.

I ran my fingers across its cool surface. It glowed faintly, in recognition. I wished I knew how to use it. I wished Ry had told me where he had gotten it, why he had chosen a Tiffany's box to keep it in, what it all meant.

I closed the lockbox, then closed the Tiffany's box, and retied the ribbon, like I'd done dozens of times over the years. I put the gun on the top shelf of my closet, then closed that door. If only it were that easy to put the gun out of my mind as well.

Something had caused the second gun to come to me. Something had powered it. Something—or someone.

I wouldn't know what until I knew more about the guns themselves.

I grabbed my cell to call Dane. Then decided I wasn't going to speak to him on the phone.

I would go to him, wherever that was.

I took my gloves off the occasional table and let myself out of the apartment, using the edges of my magic to track Dane.

It wasn't hard.

He was at the precinct, at his desk—which, I was certain—was not where he wanted to be.

———

The limestone façade of the three-story precinct building looked dirty against the sleet-shiny snow. Ry used to call it the Home of the Enemy, but he didn't really mean it. He was always mad at Dane for refusing to acknowledge the magic or the work Ry and I were doing.

The rivalry between them didn't mask the love they had for each other, though, and I knew Dane had been as torn up over Ry's death as I was.

I let myself inside, the smell of fear and sweat enveloping me. I took the steps up to the detective unit, and slipped inside.

Nighttime made little difference. There were always detectives poring over files, tapping on ancient computers, or talking tiredly into the phones.

Dane was sitting at his desk toward the back, hands pressed against his cheeks, staring down at some paperwork in front of him. His suit coat was hanging over the back of his chair, and his long dress coat was hanging on a peg on the wall.

I walked over to him and hovered, waiting for him to acknowledge me.

"At least fifteen different skin types," he said. "And they're just estimating. Who does that?"

He sounded tired. I guess the possibly special woman hadn't waited for him after all.

"Not who," I said. "*What* does that?"

"Yeah, some kinda animal," he said more to himself than to me. Because we both knew that he was deliberately misunderstanding me.

It was a good question, though. Demons shredded skin, but they used the unbelievable pain from the process to increase their own power. There were lots of creatures from all sides of the magical divide that consumed skin, mostly as food, and a handful that took the magic from tattoos.

But nothing native to New York. Because all of the native creatures destroyed the skin when they did what they did.

I knew of nothing that took tattoos like trophies.

"Was everything—" I couldn't bring myself to say skin fragments. "—tattooed?"

"Yeah," he said quietly. "Mean something to you?"

I shook my head, but he wasn't looking up. Maybe he took my silence as an acknowledgement.

"Do you know where Ry got the gun?" I asked.

Dane finally raised his head. He seemed to have aged years in the past few hours. He seemed surprised by the question.

"There were two," he said. "They belonged to my parents. I figured he had given one to you."

My cheeks heated. I had never told Dane about the gun. I hadn't told anyone.

Dane was frowning. "He was going to—you know—ask you to marry him. He was all goofy about it. He even found a Tiffany's box, because engagement rings come in Tiffany boxes. He thought you'd get it."

I thought we didn't believe in marriage. I thought marriage was so...middle class, so ostentatious.

I had missed the point.

Why me? I had asked Ry.

Because I love you, he had said, so sure, so certain.

And then, at my confusion, he had shrugged, said he was cold, and we'd better hurry. Still, we handfasted me to the gun. *My* gun. And his matched.

Like wedding rings.

Son of a bitch.

"Did your parents have wedding rings?" I asked.

"Oh, yeah," Dane said, "but my folks were pretty traditional. They wanted the guns to go to me and Ry, like we were supposed to split up the rings."

Dane leaned back, closed his eyes for a minute, shook his head, then added, "I was the only sane one. The only one who didn't see little sparklies in the universe or dark things crawling out of corners. My folks were so disappointed..."

Then he rocked forward and opened his eyes.

"I thought you knew," he said again, but I wasn't sure if he was talking about the guns or his parents or all of it.

I shrugged, pretending at a nonchalance I didn't feel. "What were the guns for?"

"Monster hunting," he said sarcastically.

I nodded, not going there.

"Thanks," I said, and threaded my way through the desks.

"Hey," he said. "You need help?"

Not your kind of help, I nearly said. Instead, I shook my head. "You guys are doing it all."

And as I walked out, I realized that was true. After I had come to my senses, I left the investigation in the hands of the police.

Even when I had known that whatever killed Ry hadn't been human—at least, by my definition. Maybe by Dane's.

But not by mine.

———

The guns had history, and I needed to find it. I could look in moldy books or try to find something accurate online. Or I could ask the guns themselves.

I didn't want to ask the one with Ry's tattoo wrapped around its grip. I wasn't sure who or what would answer me.

And I didn't want to find out.

So I walked back to my apartment, and got my gun down a second time.

Everyone describes silver as cold, but it's not. Especially when it's been indoors, and the endless winter continued outside. The gun was warm against my hand, the silver never needing polish.

I wrapped my hand around it, saw—

Ry, grinning as he watched me open the box...

I made that image disappear, saw—

Something huge and scaly, looming over a pair of sleeping boys, then

47

a bright white light zinging out of the muzzle, and the huge, scaly thing exploding into a thousand little pieces...

I shook my head, smiled a little, saw —

Hands with two matching rings, clasped, each around the grip of a different gun. "With my heart, I hold you," a male voice so like Ry's said. "With my soul, I touch you..."

It was a handfasting ceremony, only of a kind I'd never heard of. With the guns in the middle.

Marriage, the old-fashioned way.

I rubbed my eyes with my thumb and forefinger. Then frowned, thought of an experiment, and decided to try it.

I set the gun on top of the box.

Then I went into my kitchen, and thought, *Join your handfast partner* at the gun itself.

After five minutes, it wobbled its way toward me, muzzle pointed at my heart, trembling like Ry's gun had.

Find your box, I thought, and the gun wobbled its way out the door. I followed it, as it returned to the very place it had started.

I picked the box up and wrapped my arms around it.

Anniversaries had power.

I had thought the gun came to me at the anniversary of Ry's death.

The gun had come to me at the anniversary of our love—the marriage he had tried to give me, ten long years ago.

———

With my gun in my shoulder holster, I went back to the office.

I doubted I would ever get warm, even though I was wearing my coat, thick gloves, and my hat. I was cradled in the heart of a long, cold winter, and I might as well embrace it.

Ry's gun was inside the safe, the remains of my favorite tattoo still attached to the grip.

First, I put my gun on the desk. Then, gingerly, I picked up Ry's.

He laughed.

I took my hand off the grip, shaking.

Then touched it again.

I don't care how dark things get, he said. *We'll always have each other.*

As if he hadn't left. As if he were still here.

I set the guns beside each other, and they started to glow. If they were real guns—real as in the way Dane defined guns—I would be fleeing now, expecting some kind of weird explosion.

But I was curiously unafraid.

The guns glowed and locked to each other. The tattoo grew into an entire man.

Ryder.

See-through, but there.

"I missed you," he said.

I didn't care if he was real or not. "I missed you too."

"I wasn't sure you'd understand," he said. "We never finished the ceremony."

"I know," I said.

He nodded, reached toward me, his hand going through my face. I felt nothing, not even a rush of wind.

And oh, how I wanted to.

"What happened?" I asked, because I had to, because I had a sense time was short.

"Demons," he said, and his image flickered.

He glanced at the guns. The glow was fading.

"No," I said.

"I love you," he said.

"I love you too," I said. "Stay."

"I wish." His voice was faint. "Balance the scales…"

And then he was gone.

Again.

The son of a bitch.

———

I felt it—the batshit crazy. It was coming back, or maybe it had never left. I could go after everything, clean up everything, fight everything—and be consumed.

Or I could stand up.

Fight.

Figure it out.

The guns didn't glow any more. The tattoo was gone.

I touched Ry's gun. It was cool. So was mine.

Balance the scales.

Demons—and skin.

I let out a breath, grabbed both guns, and headed to the alley below.

———

No crime scene tape. No footprints in the snow. No tire marks where the crime scene unit had parked their van.

The brick was back in place.

I walked to it, touched it, felt edges, still there. The hiding place, still there.

Son of a bitch.

"Finally," he said, his voice echoing between the buildings.

I turned. He looked bigger, eyes glowing ever so slightly red, Ry's face covering his imperfectly, five tattoos glowing on his scaly skin.

Saw—in my mind's eye—two boys, sleeping, a demon hovering over them, exploding in the dark, and scales raining down—on the oldest boy, the one closest to the door.

"Your parents took your magic away from you," I said.

"They thought they could," Dane said, his voice deeper, more echoey. "They took the wrong magic."

They took the good magic, leaving the scales.

Balance them, Ry had told me.

"You killed him," I said.

Dane didn't answer me, but the tattoos glowed. The death hadn't been intentional. I knew that, or Dane wouldn't have crumbled like he had. They had had a fight—over the guns?

"What do the guns have to do with it?" I asked.

"One of them is mine," he said.

"Why didn't you take Ry's after he died?" I asked.

"I couldn't find it. But you found it. Thank you," he said. "Now, give it to me."

I had no other weapons. I hadn't expected to fight demons tonight. I wasn't really in the fighting and slaying business any more. Just the investigating, resolving business.

I pulled Ry's gun out of my pocket. My hand trembled as I gave the gun to Dane.

He took it, looking surprised at the ease.

"I never realized you were this logical," he said.

"You never knew me," I said. Which was fair: I never knew him either.

And I had dismissed Ry. Ry, who had called Dane "The Enemy" right from the start.

Dane grinned. "I like you, you know."

I nodded, as if I cared. He looked down at the gun, and weighed it in his hand, as if it were something precious.

Which it was.

Join your handfast partner, I whispered.

The gun in Dane's hand trembled. He held it tightly. The tattoos on him—Ry's remaining tattoos—glowed.

Then peeled off, one by one, each fastening itself around the gun.

For a moment, there were two men before me, one thinner, less substantial, the other glowing red, the gun between them.

My gun had found my hand as well—and I didn't remember grabbing it. Then I realized it had heard the same command, thought the command was its.

I knew what kind of bullets demons took, but I wasn't sure I wanted to shoot Dane—not with Ry fighting him for the gun.

They struggled, the ice melting beneath their feet, the heat of Dane's evil warming the entire alley. The gun remained between them and then—

Something popped as if a bubble had burst.

Ry staggered backwards, substantial, bleeding (bleeding!!!), and falling, holding his gun.

Dane, dripping scales, reached for the gun and without thinking, I imagined white light—bullets—heading toward him.

They did, shooting out of my gun and hitting his torso.

I reached down, grabbed Ry, pulled him backwards with me, away from the white-and-red glowing demon-man in the center of that alley. We made it behind a stupid snowplow-created pile of snow when Dane exploded, bits raining everywhere.

Except on us.

Balance the scales.

Not just the scales of justice. The scales of a demon, returning where they belonged.

I wrapped my arms around a bleeding, warm, *living* man.

"Ry," I said.

"Took you long enough," he muttered.

"You didn't explain—"

"No excuses," he said, and then he passed out.

———

I had no story for the ambulance attendants. I had no story for the cops. I pled ignorance, lost memory, frostbite…I don't know. Those lies are gone, along with any trace of Dane.

Ry thinks Dane died that night ten years ago, and somehow his demon self managed to get to Ry, so that Ry's power would keep them alive.

But I think—the magic suggests it—that Dane died a lot longer ago than that. Maybe the night of the demon attack, the ones the gun stopped.

Because demons can create hallucinations, images, visions, like the crime scene. How easy for one boy to die and feed a dying demon, keeping it alive, just barely, waiting for the right opportunity to grow into something stronger.

From the moment I met him, Ry said he distrusted Dane. I thought that strange for brothers. But it wasn't. It was the man reacting to something he barely remembered from his own childhood.

Ry doesn't agree.

But it doesn't matter.

Because we've done purges. We've saged the entire alley. We've warded it and cleansed it. We invited old friends to do the same.

Dane's gone.

And Ry's here.

And it's no hallucination or vision.

The most romantic gift anyone's ever given me was a gun. And a handfast.

And a future.

Together.

At last.

THE TIME COP

PATRICK ALAN MAMMAY

I am a sucker for what I call "whacked-out science fiction." You know, the kind of story that takes a standard science fiction premise, stands it on end, and then kicks it across the room. I just love that kind of story and hope to have them regularly in these pages.

Patrick Alan Mammay, in this original and really whacked-out story, takes a standard mystery detective, you know the type, then sends him a little over the top. Well, maybe a lot over the top, and then smacks the poor guy solidly into a standard, but very twisted, science fiction idea to get one of the most head-shaking stories I have read in a while.

You know, a typical Pulphouse *story.*

———

Detective Michael Walens paused outside, took a deep breath and grasped the claw-shaped handle of the door to the Big Lobster restaurant. He could tell this wasn't going to be an ordinary day. He pulled the door open and stepped inside.

"Oh, good. You're here."

Mike's eyes took a moment to adjust from the afternoon sun to the indoor fluorescent lighting. A girl sat on the bench with her hands clasped over her nose and mouth, staring forward. The restaurant smelled heavily of fried fish. The pimply teenage host with jet black hair, in that awful just woke up long spike, approached Mike.

"I'm Evan." The boy held his hand out.

Mike glanced at the hand then pulled out his notepad.

"I'm detective Walens," said Mike, looking over the freaky kid. "Who is the manager?"

Evan's hand dangled limply for a moment.

"Oh, um, ok. I'll go get her." Evan turned and scooted to find his manager, arms dangling limply at his sides.

Mike and the girl on the bench were the only two people left in the reception area. It was a small section with benches for about fifteen people and another fifteen to stand.

The bar was off to the right. Mike glanced in—empty, except for the bartender wiping the bar off.

"You ok?" Mike said to the girl on the bench. She stopped staring at the big lobster tank for a moment to look at Mike. She shook her head no, keeping her hands clasped over her nose and mouth.

The big lobster tank caught his attention. It wasn't just low on lobsters; it was low on water, too. Practically empty. Seven lobsters meandered about in just enough water to cover them.

"What's wrong?"

The manager came bustling into the room, Evan trailing behind her, limp-armed still.

"Oh, good. You're here. We're out of lobsters," said the woman in the slightly too tight white dress shirt and formerly black cotton pants, which squeezed her waist around the fifteen pounds of bulge.

"Excuse me?"

"That's where they were stolen from," said the manager, looking at the lobster tank. Evan nodded in confirmation.

"Could I have your name, ma'am." It was a statement, not a question.

"Oh. I'm Linda Doughtery. I am the assistant manager. I was on duty, but in the kitchen when it happened."

Evan pointed toward the kitchen to help illustrate where Linda was.

The girl was watching all three of them now.

"Ok, exactly what happened?"

"Someone stole all our lobsters. Look over here. I think they left a finger print on the glass. You should call in CSI."

Mike ignored that. Too many people watch unrealistic TV shows these days and think they know how to be a detective.

"How?"

"They just reached in and grabbed them all," said Linda.

Something wasn't making any sense to Mike. "They just reached in? And no one said anything? How many did they take?"

Linda looked at Evan. "What did we figure out? Twenty-seven?"

Evan nodded.

Mike blinked in shock. "Someone took twenty-seven lobsters and no one stopped them or said anything?"

"She's the only one who saw anything," chimed Evan. Linda nodded.

The girl just shook her head.

Mike pointed to the video camera above his head, aimed directly at the lobster tank.

Linda's eyes opened wide with shock as she slapped her forehead. "Oh, my God! I didn't even think of that."

———

It's not a lobster hole, you moron, it's a wormhole. Stop calling it that." Rob placed the last of the lobsters into the large trash bin filled with water, then sat down at his computer.

The top floor above ground, the fifth floor, of the Secret Underground DARPA Research Complex, SUDReC, held the four Plasma Wave Atom Smasher labs. Even though they were above ground, the labs were still considered secret.

The windowless walls of each lab were lead-lined concrete over two feet thick. The rooms were cooled by massive air conditioners, with extra fans strewn about the floor to push the air to where the vents weren't reaching.

The hum of the fans and whoosh of the vents battled the

buzzing of the Plasma Wave Atom Smasher to see which could make more noise.

"It's a hole which lobsters keep coming out of, therefore it is a lobster hole," said Armen.

Armen held his hands in his white lab coat pockets to keep it from billowing out as he walked closer to look at the monitor screen with Rob.

"What? You think I should keep saying *the wormhole in lab two where the lobsters came from*?"

"Well, it would be more accurate," said Rob, the portly scientist. "I'm just amazed that we might have solved world hunger with wormholes. I never would have put those together as a possibility." Rob looked up from the monitor for a moment.

"Promise me that you won't try to go into this one." Armen looked at Rob very sternly.

"I wanted to see if I could reach any more lobsters. They had rubber bands on their claws."

"How did you know that it was a two-way lobster hole? Your hand could have been vaporized."

"Oh, come on. One-way wormholes are just a stupid plot device. Please. Like there's any real science that suggests a one-way *wormhole*."

Rob tapped a few keys on the keyboard.

"Plus, wouldn't you want to go to an alternate universe that was filled with lobsters that already had rubber bands on their claws?"

"We don't even know if it's an alternate universe! Are you opening the wormhole again?"

"Yep. I got an idea of how we can tell if it's an alternate universe. And we can get more lobsters."

"Rob!" Armen leaned in front of Rob's monitor to give him an intense stare. "We have to discuss the ethics of taking lobsters from an alternate parallel universe!"

Rob leaned away from Armen's too close face, with a disgusted look. "How do you know we're not wealthy lobster farmers in another universe that plan to feed all the other alternate universes? I can picture a universe where I would do that. Can't you?"

Armen glanced upward, consideringlyish. I just made up that word to describe his look. Kinda makes sense, right?

"Well, yeah, I guess I probably could."

The corners of the room were filled with pairs of blade server racks, tall black metal cabinets which held rows of pizza box shaped computers wired together for parallel processing to control the Plasma Wave Atom Smasher.

Rob triumphantly hit enter on his keyboard.

The atom smasher itself was a giant tubular ring. The tube was about four feet in diameter and the track of the ring took it around the entire room, about 38 feet in diameter. Every four feet of the ring was a large rectangular block which acted as both a stand and as the plasma wave generator.

At the mid-point of the room, just off center from the circle were two bridges about three feet apart, which spanned from one side of the ring to the other.

"So, what's the plan?" asked Armen. "You aren't just grabbing more lobsters."

"Definitely more lobsters," said Rob over the rising noise of the room. "But, you'll see. I will conclusively prove this is an alternate universe."

The hum of the PWAS roared to life, a shrill high-pitched squeal joined the loud buzz as the plasma waved through the ring.

For visual effect, the two world renowned secret scientists had placed neon lights on the top and sides of the ring that blinked on and off in sequence to appear as if they were spinning around the ring as well. It looked cool, but had no bearing on the plasma wave within.

The lights continued to dim for effect as the PWAS settled into a steady "whum—whum—whum" as the neon lights circled the ring faster and faster. Across the two bridges, electrical surges sparked, arcing between the bridges, and a wispy smoke appeared.

"There it is." Rob grabbed Armen's shoulder, pointing at the arcing between the two bridges. The smoke had begun to swirl and the flat black hole began to open.

"Yes, but what's the plan?"

"Oh. You'll see! It's brilliant."

A loud boom rocked the room. The wormhole between the two bridges stabilized at three feet in diameter. A small splash of water dripped onto the lab floor from the lobster hole.

Rob and Armen stood, staring, with their ears ringing and hands clasped over them.

"Did you see that?"

"What? I can't hear anything. My ears are ringing!"

Rob grabbed an iPhone off the desk and threw it into the wormhole.

"My phone!" shouted Armen. He glared at Rob, appalled.

"Brilliant, right?" smiled Rob.

Armen grabbed Rob's phone from the desk and awkwardly flung it into the wormhole. "There. How do you like that?"

Rob was apoplectic. "You idiot! I don't have a waterproof case!"

"So?" shouted Armen.

"I sent your phone through because it had a waterproof case! Don't you get it?"

"No. You just threw my phone into an alternate universe." Armen crossed his arms, equally as furious. "So I threw yours, too."

"Yeah, now log into Find My Phone. Moron," declared Rob.

"I don't have Find My Phone enabled," said Armen. "Now who's the moron?"

————

Mike stood in the small manager's office of Big Lobster, looking over the shoulder of Linda at the four small black and white closed circuit monitors.

"Sorry, I've never really used this," said Linda, frantically looking through the manual.

The tiny desk was overrun with papers, the walls covered in corkboard with pink, yellow, and green post-it notes thumbtacked all over. Evan stood a little too close in the doorway, trying to see around Mike.

In the bottom corner monitor, Mike noticed a swirling black hole in the lobster tank, with wisps of smoke rising from it. An arm reached through, groping for the last of the lobsters.

Mike took off running, dodging around the corner of the office, past the freezer, back toward the lobby.

Without breaking stride, "Backup, send backup," Mike yelled, pressing the talk button on his shoulder radio. Mike dove through the wormhole.

Mike slid onto the floor of the fourth floor lab of the SUDReC building.

"I can't reach the phhho— Holy crap! A time-space traveler!"

Armen turned to see what Rob was talking about.

"It's just like Led Zeppelin said in Kashmir," said Rob.

"What?" asked Armen.

Mike leapt to his feet and drew his sidearm. "Freeze, hands where I can see them," Mike shouted over the fans. He tried to look around the room, in case there were any other aliens.

"He's a Time Cop!" exclaimed Armen.

"But the prophecy said—," said Rob.

Armen eyed Rob sideways. "That's a Zeppelin song."

"They were prophets."

"Where am I?" shouted Mike. "Hands up!"

Rob and Armen both put their hands up.

"Did we break some sort of space time law, officer?" said Armen.

"What? No? What—what is that thing and where am I? Who are you and how come I can understand you?" Mike was very confused.

Evan's pimply head poked through the wormhole.

"Officer Walens?" called Evan, as he looked around, eyes adjusting and finally seeing Mike. "Take my hand and I'll pull you back!" Evan's hand appeared, followed by an arm, then a shoulder.

"Evan?" said Rob.

"Uncle Rob? Oh, hey, Uncle Rob. What are you doing on this alien ship?"

"This is my lab, what are you doing in my wormhole?"

"I'm trying to save officer Walens."

Mike shook his head, trying to wake up from whatever bizarre nightmare he was having.

"Evan, either come in or get out, before the lobster hole collapses and rips you in half," said Armen, motioning for him to get out.

Evan started to duck back then paused. "Are you coming Officer Walens?"

"No, not until I get the lobsters. You get out of here." Mike holstered his weapon as Evan sank back through. "Ok, you two start explaining."

"Evan, throw our phones back!" shouted Rob to his disappearing nephew.

Two phones clattered onto the floor before the wormhole collapsed with a loud 'bampf' sound.

"You're not a time cop?" said a disappointed Armen.

"I'm an officer from the Tulsa Police Department looking for some missing lobsters from Big Lobster."

Rob dejectedly pointed at the water-filled trash can in the corner. "I guess we're not solving world hunger this way, but it does explain the rubber bands."

"What?"

"We still don't know if he's from a parallel universe or not," said Armen.

"I'll call Evan," said Rob.

Mike looked into the lobster can. "Are all of them here?"

"Yeah," admitted Armen. "We did have a couple picked out for lunch, but didn't get a chance to eat them yet."

Rob hung up the phone dejectedly. "Well, I guess you're from our timeline. Evan wants to know when you're coming back."

"Do you have a business card, officer?" Armen held out his hand. "We might need you as the first Time Cop at some point. You have more experience than anyone else."

"Van Damme was the first Time Cop."

"Yeah, but Jet Li was The One!"

Mike slid the trash can over to the middle of the room. "Just get me out of here and we'll pretend this never happened. Especially the last part where you didn't mention Dr. Who, Bill or Ted."

CATASTROPHE BAKER AND
THE COLD EQUATIONS

MIKE RESNICK

Mike is the all-time leading award winner in science fiction short stories. He has been nominated for a record thirty-seven Hugo Awards for his work. Yes, he's won a bunch as well.

On top of the all the novels and short stories, Mike is also an editor, including over forty anthologies in which he bought a number of stories from me over the years. Right now he is editing Galaxy's Edge Magazine *as well as* Stellar Guild Books.

Just like Mike's story in Issue Zero, for those of you who know the history of science fiction, this wonderful story will have an extra level. But even if you don't know the history, the story is a great romp. Have fun.

If you really want to know about the cold equations, there's only one person to ask, and that's me—Catastrophe Baker, hero by trade but all too frequently fugitive by misunderstanding.

It all began one night back on Tombstone III, the second planet in the New Arizona system. (Yeah, I know it says III, but it was named before that crazy Professor McNally blew Tombstone II to bits trying to make the Perfect Vodka Martini in his lab.)

Anyway, I was just kind of unwinding in the local tavern with a bottle of Antarean brandy, and trying to figure out what to drink next after the last of it was gone, which figgered to be mighty soon, when a burly bearded man walked right up to me and tried to shove his nose up against mine, which would have worked better if he hadn't been a little feller who was only three or four inches over six feet.

"Catastrophe Baker," he said kind of irritably, "I been looking for you far and wide."

"Well, friend," I replied, "maybe you should have been looking for me high and low. Mostly high."

He didn't so much as crack a smile, which convinced me right off that he didn't have no sense of humor.

"Catastrophe Baker," he said, "are you going to marry my daughter or not?"

"Who's your daughter?" I asked.

"Fatima Muldoon."

"Cute little Fatima?" I said, trying to imagine how something that round and pretty and friendly could be related to this here feller. "Did she send you here on this mission of matchmaking?"

"She did not," he said. "She's sitting in her room, crying her poor little heart out." He glared at me. "You can't leave her like that. Promises were made."

"I promised her a night of heavenly rapture," I replied, wrapping my dignity around me like a cloak, "and I delivered on it. Marriage wasn't never mentioned."

"What have you got against my daughter?" he demanded. "Why won't you marry her?"

"Marriage just don't go with the heroing trade, Friend Muldoon," I said. "I'm always on the move, and most of the innocent young damsels I rescue just can't be held back from thanking me in meaningful ways." I paused for a minute whilst he digested what I said, because it was true that being a hero could tire you out more than the general public ever imagined. "Why not have a drink and forget the whole thing?" I concluded.

"Not a chance, you foul blaggard!" he said, picking up my glass and throwing its contents in my face.

I realized he was just a distraught and loving father, so I didn't do much more than bust his ribs and break his left leg and knock out fourteen of his teeth as a gentle reproof. I'd have offered him a drink again, but it was pretty obvious that he planned to spend the rest of his time in the tavern just lying there on the floor, moaning and twitching.

Nobody else said much of anything, but I noticed they all

gave me a wide berth on their way out, and in fact the whole place was empty in less than a minute, except for me and the barkeep and Muldoon. I was just about to order myself a bottle of Cygnian cognac when three men entered the tavern, all of 'em wearing glowing police badges on their chests.

"Boy!" said the one on the left, staring at Muldoon. "You sure didn't leave much that don't need work."

"I seen guys what got caught in machine mangles and came away looking better than this poor bastard," agreed the one on the right.

"That's enough, you two," said the one in the middle. "Catastrophe Baker, I'm here to arrest you for disturbing the peace."

"Disturbing the peace?" moaned Muldoon, though it was kind of hard to understand him, what with him missing all them teeth. "He damned near killed me!"

"Don't interrupt!" said the one in the middle. "I'm the Chief of Police on Tombstone III, and I'm still sorting out what happened."

"How come you're Chief of Police?" I asked.

"You don't think I fit the job?" he said, his hand hovering over his pulse gun.

"Sure you do," I said. "But shouldn't a place called Tombstone have a town marshal instead of a police chief?"

"You know, now that you mention it, it does seem a lot more fitting, doesn't it?"

"Sure," I said. "And these two guys could be called your deputies."

"I like that," said the Chief.

"Isn't anyone going to call the hospital?" wailed Muldoon.

"Don't interrupt when we're discussing police business!" snapped the Chief.

"I'm bleeding to death!" said Muldoon.

"Oh, don't be such a baby," said the Chief. "That's hardly

more than a pint or two of blood on the floor." He turned back to me. "You got a good head on your shoulders, Catastrophe Baker. How'd you like to come to work for the Tombstone Marshall's office?"

"If you're the Marshall you're supposed to arrest him!" wailed Muldoon. "Or better still, shoot him!"

"One more word out of you, Jebediah Muldoon," said the Chief, "and I'm tossing you in jail for disturbing the peace."

"Get me a transfusion first and I'll be happy to go," said Muldoon.

The Chief turned to his deputies. "Get him something to drink and see if that shuts him up."

"And a straw," moaned Muldoon.

The Chief—well, I suppose I might as well start calling him the Marshall, since that's what he began calling himself—turned to me.

"So what do you think?" he said.

"I appreciate the offer," I said, "but when you're a bona fide hero like me, you can't confine yourself to one planet. There's voluptuous young damsels all over the galaxy what need rescuing, and of course there's would-be Galactic Emperors to capture and there's always a Pirate Queen or two what needs taming, and besides, no insult intended, but Tombstone's got the worst-stocked bars for light-years in any direction."

"You make being a hero sound exciting as all hell," said the Marshall kind of enviously.

"Well, it is," I agreed. "Except for the parts where I get shot at or tortured."

"What were you doing on Tombstone, anyway?" he asked.

"Ruining my daughter and killing her father!" moaned Muldoon.

"If you can't lie still and stop interrupting, I'm gonna add ten days to your sentence," said the Marshall.

Suddenly we heard some screams from down the street, and I could see the glare of laser beams against the black of night.

"Looks like somebody got into a fight down at Sleepy Joe's Emporium," said one of the deputies. "Couple of 'em are firing their burners, and another one just shot up the grocery store with his pulse gun."

"I wonder," said the Marshall, ignoring the distraction. "You think Sheriff might be a better title?"

A couple of more screams came our way.

"Chief, they're starting to shoot each other instead of inanimate buildings!" said the deputy.

"Good," said the Marshall. "Them buildings are hard to replace." He turned back to me. "So what do you think— Marshall or Sheriff?"

"Chief!" yelled the other deputy. "They're burning Sleepy Joe's down to the ground!"

"Didn't your mama teach you no manners?" demanded the Chief. "You're interrupting a vitally important business conversation." He paused to get his temper under control. "What do you say, Catastrophe Baker?"

"Well, now," I said thoughtfully, "Marshall's got eight letters and Sheriff's only got seven, so I reckon that makes Marshall more important."

"Dessicated corpse got more letters than any of 'em," groaned Muldoon.

"You know," said the Marshall, "if we don't get him to a doctor pretty soon, I'm gonna finish what you started."

"Okay, I was on my way out of here anyway," I said. "I'll just heft him up on my shoulder and toss him off at the first doctor's office I come to."

"You stay away from me!" yelled Muldoon, curling himself up in a little ball.

I picked him up, tossed him maybe ten feet in the air, and

while he was stretched out, pawing at empty space and screaming like a banshee, I caught him on my shoulder. All the air kind of rushed out of him, but since I'd already broke his ribs I don't imagine it could have done them much more harm.

"What in the world was this all about anyway?" asked the Marshall as I headed for the door.

"I had carnival knowledge with his daughter," I said.

"With sweet innocent little Fatima?" he said.

"Yeah."

"You ought to be ashamed of yourself," said the Marshall sternly. Suddenly he learned forward. "How was she?"

I pulled myself up to my full height, which was just a shade under seven feet. "A gentleman never discusses such things." Which was absolutely true. Personally, I always figgered it was so he wouldn't inadvertently give away no pointers.

Then I was out the door and walking down the street. I felt right good about the thought of leaving Tombstone, which added a little bounce to my step, and the way I knew it was because Muldoon gave out an agonized moan with each step I took.

I couldn't find no doctor's office open, but there was a veterinarian with a light in his window down at the end of the street, so I toted Muldoon over there.

"I'm no doctor, I'm a veterinarian," said the vet when I unloaded my burden onto his examining table.

"He keeps screaming for a doctor, and since no one wants to listen to him clear through til morning, I figger you're the next best thing. Just patch him up and then turn him over to the jail."

"I've got no problem turning him over to the jail," said the vet. "It's the patching him up that's going to be tricky."

"You sew up animals, don't you?" I said encouragingly.

"The mutated cattle out on the farms," he said. "But only after I castrate 'em."

Muldoon kind of whimpered and curled up in a little ball

again.

"That seems kind of a harsh cure," I allowed. "Don't you know how to do nothing else?"

"I suppose I could nail some shoes on him and put a ring in his nose," offered the vet.

"Take me back to the bar and beat the crap out of me!" rasped Muldoon. "I was safer there!"

"I can see where the man could really get to be a nuisance to have around," said the vet. "I suppose castrating him would calm him down and kind of gentle him out."

"He's already added to Nature's game plan with a lovely little lady that won my heart, at least for an evening," I said. "I don't suppose he'd miss 'em all that much."

"He wouldn't have to miss them at all," said the vet. "I could give him a little glass jar to carry them around in. Maybe he could hang the jar around his neck on a string."

"Now that'd be a surefire attention-getter next time he walked into a bar," I said.

"Or better still," said the vet, "he could hang them from the ring I'm putting in his nose."

"Man, he ain't never gonna run out of conversational ice breakers," I said enthusiastically. "I'm sure glad we ran into you, and I know that once Muldoon gets over his little fit of pique and heals from whatever agonies of the damned you're gonna put him through, he'll be everlastingly grateful."

"Speaking of the patient," said the vet, "where is he?"

I looked around and damned if the examining table wasn't empty. I couldn't find Muldoon hiding under none of the furniture, of which there wasn't an awful lot in the first place, and then I chanced to look out the door, and I saw him crawling due north down the middle of the street, paying no attention at all to any of the traffic that kept barely missing him.

"Look at him go!" said the vet admiringly. "Hell, I've got

herding dogs that don't travel as fast on all fours."

"I guess he didn't need patching up as bad as he thunk he did," I said. "Too bad. You'd have turned him into one hell of a conversation piece."

"Well, we all have to learn to live with disappointment," he said, taking it all philanthropically.

Truer words was never spoke, because when I went to the spaceport to get into my ship and take off for parts known, who should be waiting for me with their weapons drawn but the Marshall and his deputies.

"Catastrophe Baker," he said, "I'm putting you under arrest."

"What for this time?" I asked.

"You double-parked your spaceship."

"You can't double-park a spaceship," I told him.

"Are you calling me a liar?" he said. "I'm the Marshall, and if I say you double-parked it, you double-parked it. The fine is seventeen gazillion credits, payable immediately."

I reached into my pocket and pulled out everything I found.

"Will you settle for twenty-seven credits, three Maria Theresa dollars, and a fish hook?" I asked.

"That'll make an acceptable down payment," he said, grabbing it from me. "We'll let you work the rest of it off."

"I ain't much on math," I said, "but even at a thousand credits a day, it's gonna take me a couple of months to work off seventeen gazillion of 'em ."

"This is your lucky day, Catastrophe Baker!" he cried enthusiastically. "I just happen to know of a job that pays seventeen gazillion credits, minus twenty-seven credits and three Maria Theresa dollars, whatever the hell that comes to."

"Doing what?" I said.

"Almost nothing at all," he said.

"I like it already," I said. "What particular kind of nothing does this job entail?"

"I just want you to fly to Godwin II, about eighty light years from here, over in the Quinellus Cluster."

"No problem," I said, taking a step toward my ship. "I'll start right now."

"Not so fast," he said, and suddenly I was looking down the barrels of three laser pistols again. "First we got to load the cargo."

"It ain't a real big ship," I said. "Just a one-man job. What kind of cargo are you talking about?"

"Desperately-needed medication for the colonists on Godwin II," he said. "It ain't all that heavy. We'll stick a few boxes in your cargo hold in the next couple of minutes and you can be on your way."

"I ain't got no cargo hold," I said.

"Sure you do. Of course, you call it a closet, but we already emptied out all your clothes and trinkets, so now it's a cargo hold."

"I may need them clothes in the future," I said, starting to feel a tad riled.

"You'll buy new ones," said the Marshall.

"With what?" I demanded.

"Have you forgotten you're being paid seventeen gazillion credits?" he said. "You'll be a rich man when you land."

Well, I hadn't looked at it that way before, but it made sense when he spelled it out for me, so I agreed to take the job, and spent the next five minutes in the spaceport bar while his men loaded the medication.

"One last thing," said the Marshall as he walked me out to the ship. "This stuff ain't no good if the temperature gets down under sixty degrees Fahrenheit, even for a few seconds, so don't land anywhere near the polar caps."

I told him I wouldn't forget, and then a couple of minutes later I closed and locked the hatch, and took off. I figured the trip would take maybe two days at full speed and traversing the right wormholes, but I just turned it over to Bubbles, which is what I call the navigational computer, mostly because she's got a nice ladylike voice, and I didn't pay it no never-mind for the next couple of hours. In fact, I was watching some uplifting holographic entertainments featuring young ladies what was dressed for extremely warm weather when Bubbles suddenly turned off the show.

"What's going on?" I said.

"I wish I could shake your hand, kiss you good-bye, and tell you to be brave, but I'm only a computer," said Bubbles. "Something has gone terribly wrong with your mission."

"It ain't a mission," I explained. "It's just a trip to Godwin II."

"At our current rate of speed, you will arrive in six days and three hours."

"You got it all wrong," I said. "This here flight figures to take another day and a half."

"Not under current conditions," said Bubbles. "And in twenty-seven minutes I will be unable to maintain a cabin temperature of sixty degrees."

"If you got a leak, fix it," I said, getting mighty annoyed at this interruption, because the young ladies were about to dance to a strain of classical drum music and I didn't want to miss such a highbrow entertainment.

"I do not have a leak."

"Okay, then, if you have a fuel blockage, fix it."

"I do not have a fuel blockage," said Bubbles.

"I give up," I said. "What do you have?"

"A stowaway."

"Yeah? Where?"

"I have no cargo hold, no separate sleeping cabin, and a single closet," said Bubbles. "Even you should be able to figure that one out."

"Go back to running the ship," I said. "I'll take it from here."

I walked over and flang open the closet, and sitting on top of a bunch of boxes was the most beautiful lady I ever did see. What she was wearing didn't have hardly enough material to make a handkerchief. She had a burner and a screecher in holsters that were bonded to her legs, and I could see a dagger peeking out of the top of her boot.

She kind of oozed down off the boxes and stepped out into the room. Then she stretched, and I felt an urge to put my hand in front of my eyes so they wouldn't pop out, but I didn't do it because it would have spoiled the view.

"I am Zenobia," she said, licking her moist, red lips.

"That figgers," I said.

"It does?" she said kind of curiously.

"Ma'am," I answered, "Zenobia is a name what Pirate Queens just naturally seem to favor. Man and boy I've run across fourteen Pirate Queens, and counting you eleven of 'em was named Zenobia."

"What makes you think I'm a Pirate Queen?" she asked.

"Well, ma'am, in my long experience Pirate Queens can always be identified by their name, their lustful natures, their soul-destroying greed, and their proud arrogant bosoms."

She smiled the kind of smile that made me want to howl at the nearest twenty or thirty moons. "How clever of you to know."

"Ma'am, why is someone who wants to lay waste to the galaxy, plunder it six ways to Sunday, and enslave a trillion people, stowing away on my ship?"

"I was hiding from the Navy," she said. "They got word that I was on Tombstone, and I got word that they were coming after me in force."

"Well, Miss Zenobia, ma'am," I said, "I'll be happy to drop you off somewhere, once I unload the cargo that you was co-habiting my closet with."

"All I want to do is go anywhere the Navy isn't," she said. "What's your destination?"

"Godwin II."

"That's as good a world as any."

"I hate to interrupt this little lovefest," said Bubbles, who didn't sound like she hated interrupting us at all, "but the cabin temperature has dropped two degrees in the past five minutes."

"So heat it up," I said.

"I can't," said Bubbles. "It's taking all my power to produce enough air for both of you. Remember, I was originally programmed to carry just one person to Godwin II."

"I don't suppose we could take turns breathing," I said, but even I could see that it wasn't that all-fired practical an idea, because even though I was a good foot and a half taller than Zenobia, she had a bigger chest and figured to need more air than me.

"So it'll get chilly," she said. "Big deal."

"You don't understand," I said. "If it drops under sixty degrees, all that medication will spoil and I'll be out seventeen gazillion credits."

"What the hell's in those boxes?" she asked.

"Beats me," I said. "All I know is that it can't get below sixty."

"Make up your mind, Catastrophe Baker," said Bubbles. "You can have oxygen for two, or you can have a heated cabin, but you can't have both. Those," she concluded, intoning it like a high priestess or a politician, "are the cold equations."

"I'm sorry I got you into this, Catastrophe Baker," said Zenobia. "If I'd known, I'd have been happy to put off conquering the galaxy until next week."

"We ain't beat yet," I said. "We'll think of some way out of this."

"But what about the cold equations?" she asked.

"I'm working on it," I told her. "Bubbles, how long until we land on Godwin II?"

"Six days, two hours, and fifty-four minutes."

"The medication will be ruined long before then," said Zenobia.

And then it hit me. "Maybe not," I said.

"But the cold equations . . ."

"Forget 'em ," I said, starting to slip out of my duds. "You and me'll practice the *warm* equations."

I knew she'd go for it, because Pirate Queens are always ripe for generating a little heat, if you catch my subtle meaning, and no sooner had the words left my mouth than she flang her weapons to the floor and her body against mine. About ten seconds later she hit G above high C, and a minute after that she reached Q above high H, and I figgered we'd better take it easy or her screams might bust all the instruments.

But taking it easy ain't what Pirate Queens is all about. We didn't eat and we didn't sleep and we didn't talk (not in any known language, anyway), and about every five hours we'd take an hour off to rest and recuperate. But each time the cabin would get cooler and we'd go right back to work, and finally, on the fifth day I figgered I just had to have a break, but Bubbles told me that if I did the medication would spoil.

I just didn't have no energy left after five days cooped up with a healthy Pirate Queen, and I figgered that despite all our efforts the cold equations were going to carry the day, and then I figgered, well, maybe if I jettisoned half the medication, Bubbles could keep the temperature up in the low sixties for another day. So I opened the closet, ready to pull out a box and dump it, when I finally read the label, and I realized that the warm equations were going to win after all. A couple of minutes later Zenobia was hitting Z over high J again, and we were having such a good time that we didn't even stop for another hour after the ship touched down the next day.

Finally Zenobia stood up, and even after she got dressed and put on all her weaponry, she was still panting a bit and kind of red in the face. She stood by the hatch while it opened, extended her hand to me, shook mine as vigorously as you'd expect from a lady who was out to subjugate a few thousand races, and said, "Catastrophe Baker, it's been an experience."

Just six words, but she sure put her heart into them, which was only just and fitting, since she'd put everything else into the last six days. Then she was gone, and I decided it was time to unload the cargo and earn my seventeen gazillion credits.

"I hope we never see her again, the hussy," said Bubbles.

I figgered it was best not to tell her I already had a date with Zenobia for that evening, and I began hauling out the cargo.

"Thank God you have arrived!" said the governor of the little colony. "You can't imagine how badly we've needed this! Three cheers for Catastrophe Baker!" And he led all the assembled men and women in a chorus of hip-hip-hoorays.

"You're going to be half a box short," I said when the celebration had died down.

"What happened to it?" asked the Governor. "It hasn't started spoiling, has it?"

"No," I said, and then I figured I might as well put the best face on it. "I field-tested it."

"You field-tested eight hundred erectile dysfunction pills?" he asked, his eyes so wide you could see the white all around the irises.

"It's all about the cold equations," I said. "Now, you probably ain't gonna believe this, but . . ."

And I proceeded to tell him the whole story, and sure enough he didn't believe it.

But after dinner I hunted up Zenobia the Pirate Queen, and she sure did. They tossed us out of the hotel when she shattered every window from the third through the eighth floor.

TIME, EXPRESSED AS AN ENTRÉE

ROBERT JESCHONEK

For the third issue in a row I wanted to start off with a Robert Jeschonek story. In four issues of this magazine so far, he has had a story in every one.

In this story Robert takes a wild science fiction idea that spans universes and brings it down to a very, very human level. I have never seen anyone be able to do that in such a perfect fashion before.

Robert's wonderful stories have appeared in many magazines and he has published dozens of novels as well as worked for DC Comics. I would highly suggest you find some of his work if you like any of his stories here. He is an original voice in fiction.

―――――

The rainbow leviathan opened all his trillion trillion mouths at once and gobbled up the next-to-the-last day of the timeline.

Centillions of life forms screamed at once, but that was background static to the leviathan. All the time in all the universe rushed into its trillion trillion mouths with staggering force, but that was filet mignon with a side of lobster tail to the creature.

Not that filet mignon or lobster existed in this universe-which-was-not-our-own. Not that there was anything precisely like either delicacy in the milky-orange reaches of this alien space, with its red-and-white-striped sun-swarms and its planets like tangled neon tubes in constantly shifting configurations.

The last precious seconds of the next-to-the-last day gushed into the trillion trillion mouths. The "sound" it all made as it died —the simultaneous screaming of a multitude of life-forms across all frequencies, followed by the flushing of an entire universe down the gullet of the leviathan—was what the creature had taken as his name: EeePavoosh.

If the EeePavoosh—a matrix of sentient energy, subatomic strings, and gray matter—had actually had lips, he would have smacked them in satisfaction at the last bites of his food. As it was, he settled for thrashing his light-years-long shimmering rainbow tail through the infinite black void that was left in the wake of the devoured day.

Then, he turned his pale, rippling face toward his next meal. He sensed it beyond the shuddering veil of the void, glowing like a single flickering flame in a pitch-black abyss. One last taste of the timeline awaited—one last day, glittering like a perfect jewel.

The EeePavoosh had eaten all the rest, swooping like a shark through what had once been an octodecillion-year timeline, biting off every other day, year, century, and millennium. Now, he was down to one. One more feast of a day, and this timeline would be extinct.

Then what? Then nothing, perhaps. The EeePavoosh had no idea where he would go next. He had gobbled up every other adjacent timeline and could sense no others beyond this one.

Not that he was worried about that. He had been born to eat and move on, to never stop moving. He possessed a simple faith that he would somehow find more food and survive.

And so, with one last triumphant roar in the emptiness, the EeePavoosh plunged into the pristine bubble of the last remaining day.

On the other side of the veil, it was like nothing had happened to the rest of time. Space spread out in all directions, swirling with sun swarms circling planetary bodies.

The EeePavoosh's multi-frequency, infinite-range senses captured every detail of his food, judging the meal's suitability... and any irregularities that could interfere with consumption and digestion. He didn't expect to find any; he hadn't, in any of the other days he had devoured.

And yet, he found one here. He found an anomaly, something that didn't belong in what was left of this timeline and universe.

Like a bird in flight spotting one tiny worm in the earth far below, the EeePavoosh zeroed in on the anomaly and dove toward it. Rainbow tail lashing, he rode gravity waves and solar winds, crossing the sprawling universe in one tiny fraction of the one last day in which it existed.

Arriving at his destination, the EeePavoosh coasted to a stop, gazing at a planetary body of purple and yellow neon tubes. The anomaly occupied one tiny spot on the surface.

Extruding a sliver of his gargantuan body, the EeePavoosh created an avatar small enough to interact with the anomaly. Rainbow colors flickered to life along the avatar's ten-meters-long tail, and dozens of mouths flexed open and closed along its flanks.

Satisfied, the EeePavoosh rode his avatar down to the planet's surface. Emerging from a layer of pale violet clouds, he gazed down with the single multifaceted red eye that occupied most of his face and saw what he had come for. Hundreds of feet below, sitting on green-and-purple-striped stones on the bank of a bright yellow river, was the anomaly.

Specifically, it was a life form with four appendages, one head, and pink skin. Its head was topped with a soft mane that flowed midway down its back—mostly gray, streaked with dark brown.

————

The EeePavoosh came to rest near the anomaly, hovering two meters above the ground. For a long moment, the anomaly just stared silently at him with its pair of dull green eyes and its single mouth open wide.

Finally, the anomaly spoke. "Thank God I'm drunk, or this might scare the livin' crap outta me." Its mouth curled up at both corners, revealing a sparse arrangement of broken teeth. "Well, don't just hang there, buddy. Introduce yourself."

The EeePavoosh rotated slowly, considering. The sounds the

anomaly made seemed familiar. He had a feeling he had heard them before in some timeline he had devoured…but he couldn't remember where or when.

The anomaly raised one of its upper appendages and shook it back and forth. "I'm Matilda Scanlon. My friends call me Tillie." Tillie leaned forward and narrowed her eyes. "Are *you* a friend?"

The EeePavoosh thought some more, then understood. A run of connections sparked in his gargantuan memory archives, linking similar sounds, facial expressions, and gestures from various extinct species whose timelines he had eaten. None were exactly the same, but they shared enough traits that the EeePavoosh could use them to cobble together a rough translation.

More than that, the EeePavoosh could algorithmically process the commonalities into a set of responses. "Yes." He spoke from his dozens of mouths with dozens of voices, each a different pitch, timbre, and volume. "I am a friend."

Tillie let loose with a flurry of high-pitched stuttering sounds. Comparing them to similar sounds in his archives, the EeePavoosh identified them as laughter (though he didn't use that word).

"Well, it's about time you showed up, friend," said Tillie. "I was startin' to think I was alone here."

"You are not alone." The EeePavoosh's grasp of the anomaly's language was quickly improving. The more he heard of it, the better he understood.

He was also gathering other data on the anomaly. Biologically, it was similar to evolved primates from other timelines. The arrangement of its appendages was even the same as that of certain primates—two arms and two legs, ending in hands and feet which in turn ended in multiple digits. Further, the creature possessed physical traits associated in some primate species with the female gender. So Tillie, as it called itself, was a *she*.

"Let's drink to new friends." Tillie's mouth curled up at the corners again. Reaching into the folds of the loose black garment she wore, she drew out a glass container in a paper wrapper—a bottle in a bag. Unscrewing the cap, she lifted the bottle to her lips and tilted it high. A trickle of liquid flowed down into her mouth, and she swallowed it.

The EeePavoosh identified the liquid as an extract of fermented biological material. Monitoring its passage through her system, he saw it was having an effect on her body chemistry, altering the functions of certain organs. It was a phenomenon he'd observed before: intoxication, an impairment of mental and physical functions which certain species seemed to find pleasurable.

"Nice." Tillie wiped her mouth on the back of one of her hands. "I'd offer ya' some, but there's only a swig or two left. I'm thinkin' I'd better nurse it, know what I mean?" She screwed the cap back on the bottle and stuffed it in the pocket of her garment. "Unless you know where there's a package store around this joint."

"Package store?" said the EeePavoosh. "Joint?"

"If you got one of *those*, that'd be even better." Tillie's laughter started loud, then trailed off. "But y'know what, buddy? I might settle for you tellin' me where the hell I am right now." Tillie spread her arms wide, taking in her surroundings. "What is this freakin' place, anyway?"

"When," said the EeePavoosh. "The question you should ask is *when*."

"Okay then," said Tillie. "When am I right now?"

"The end of time," said the EeePavoosh.

"Huh?" Tillie scrunched her eyes and nose in what looked to the EeePavoosh like an expression of displeasure. "Are you trying to tell me I'm at the end of freakin' time?"

"The end of *this* time," said the EeePavoosh. "The last day of this existence."

"No kiddin'." Tillie shook her head. "And to think I was just in Pittsburgh an hour ago."

"Pittsburgh?" The EeePavoosh flicked his tail. "Is that a location?"

"Yeah," said Tillie. "It's on the other side of that damn thing." She pointed a finger at what looked at first like empty space. But as the EeePavoosh stared, the space rippled, revealing the outline of a transparent oval disk floating a meter above the purple ground.

Curious, the EeePavoosh trained all his senses on the disk. "The other side?"

"That's right, buddy." Tillie got up from her purple-and-green-striped rock and walked over to the disk. "I walked through it in Pittsburgh and ended up here. Some kind'a doorway, I'm guessin'." Reaching out, she pushed her arm into the oval…and it went straight through as if the oval weren't there. "A *sucky* doorway. I can't seem to go back through it."

"And you *want* to go back through?" asked the EeePavoosh.

"It's funny," said Tillie. "All my life, I wanted to get away from it all. I was just wishin' that very thing when the doorway opened up, in fact. I was homeless and sick and lonely, and I just wanted to get away. But now that I have…" She looked around at the purple and yellow landscape. "…I just want to go home again."

The EeePavoosh glided closer to the disk, picking up the faintest trace of time energy from it…just a whisper. "If it is a doorway, a portal, it is closed."

"Apparently." Tillie laughed. "Just my luck."

"Luck." The EeePavoosh drifted closer, sniffing at the time-trace. Was it a sign of a tiny temporal pocket, a bubble that would barely make a light snack for him…or something bigger?

Tillie hiked a thumb at the disk. "Don't suppose you know how to open it?"

"No." The EeePavoosh kept probing, straining to amplify the trace. "Not yet."

"Not yet?" Tillie tipped her head to one side. "So do you think you could open it eventually?"

The EeePavoosh circled around the portal, sniffing at the whispery signal it was giving off. "Not yet. But yes. I think I could."

Tillie's face brightened. "When? When could you do it?"

"Soon, I think." The EeePavoosh stopped circling and glided through the oval outline of the portal. "It requires more study, but it could be done."

"Ain't that fine and dandy!" Tillie clapped her hands. "You're going to help me? Help me get home?"

"I will open the portal," said the EeePavoosh. "I will access the other side." Even as he spoke to her, the EeePavoosh was busy measuring every characteristic of the portal. Though he had devoured an entire timeline except for one day, he was already hungry for what lay beyond the doorway.

Tillie moved a hand toward him, then caught herself and pulled it away. "Well, thank you, buddy. I'm really itchin' to go back. I was just thinkin' about it when you showed up, in fact. Prayin' about it, for what it's worth." Looking down, she kicked a purple pebble with the toe of her shoe. "Maybe I shouldn't care. I mean, I've never amounted to much. I'm sure nobody even knows I'm gone. But home is home, right?"

The EeePavoosh kept working. "Home is home," he said.

"Maybe I had to lose it to appreciate it," said Tillie. "Or maybe the Lord had a plan in store for me."

"A plan?" said the EeePavoosh.

"For my life to mean somethin'," said Tillie. "I always wanted it to, but it never did. I'm just a homeless alcoholic who can't even help herself. But maybe, comin' here like this…" She kicked another pebble. "Maybe there's still somethin' I'm supposed to do. Whatta you think?"

The EeePavoosh didn't answer.

Tillie watched him for a moment. "You're not an *angel* by any chance, are you?"

"No." The EeePavoosh wasn't sure what an angel was, but nothing in his archives made him think the term had anything to do with him.

"Well, thanks anyway for helpin' with the doorway," said Tillie. "It's been a long time since anyone's done somethin' this nice for me. A *long* time."

"A long time?" said the EeePavoosh. "How long?"

"Years and years." Tillie shook her head. "Decades, even."

"Years? Decades?" Aligning the context with similar semantic constructs from the languages in his vast memory archives, the EeePavoosh became intrigued. The way the female talked about units of time distracted him from his work.

"It's the story of my life," said Tillie. "Sixty years of bullshit, and it feels like an eternity."

"Eternity?" The thought of it distracted the EeePavoosh further. "How do sixty years feel like eternity?"

"Livin' the kind of life I've been livin'." Tillie squinted up at the lavender clouds squirming in the hot pink sky. "Days have a way of feelin' like decades."

The EeePavoosh was having trouble paying attention to his work. "All time is like this on the other side? Days feel like decades? Years feel like eternity?"

"For me, they do." Tillie scrubbed her hands through her stringy brown-and-gray mane. "Some more than others, I guess."

The phenomenon she was describing excited the EeePavoosh. Was it possible, on the other side of the portal, that time was somehow amplified? That it could be extended beyond its usual properties?

The internal structure of the EeePavoosh's avatar shivered with anticipation, and the structure of the parent leviathan in orbit around the planet did the same. "I want to know more."

"I can tell." Tillie smiled. "You're really interested in this stuff, aren't ya'?"

"I am," said the EeePavoosh.

Tillie narrowed her eyes. "Makes you wanna open that doorway faster, doesn't it? To see what's on the other side."

"It does." Even as he said it, the EeePavoosh redoubled his efforts to analyze the portal. "Now tell me more about the longer times on the other side."

Tillie nodded. "Why not, if it gets me home faster?" Pulling out the bottle in the bag, she opened and tipped it to her lips… tipped it high, almost straight up. The EeePavoosh heard a tiny trickle run into her mouth, then nothing. "Damn." Tillie lowered the bottle. "Don't suppose you could whip me up a little joy juice, couldja, buddy?"

"No joy juice," said the EeePavoosh. "Now tell me about the longer times on the other side."

Tillie pitched the bottle, and it shattered against a nearby boulder. "Where to begin?"

The EeePavoosh thought she was asking him a question. "Begin by telling me what makes time longer on the other side."

"Suffering," said Tillie. "That's what makes it longer. Like, for example, the five years I spent married to Ray Coleman. They felt more like *fifty* years than five."

"Married?" said the EeePavoosh.

"When a man and a woman get together," said Tillie, "and make each other miserable for the rest of their lives."

"How does this make time longer?" asked the EeePavoosh.

"Well, it's like this," said Tillie. "When I was a little girl, I used to dream about fallin' in love and gettin' married. I spent hours and hours imaginin' what it would be like.

"I wanted a big, strong man to save me...to take me away from home, so my daddy couldn't get me anymore. And the funny thing is, I got one. A big, strong man." Tillie shook her head. "And he proceeded to kick my ass six ways from Sunday. I went from *one* man abusin' me to *another*."

"This kicking your ass," said the EeePavoosh. "It made the time longer?"

"Longer than you can imagine," said Tillie. "Every day felt like a year. The pain...the helplessness." She sniffed and dabbed at the corners of her eyes. "But the worst part, the longest, was the *waiting*. Waiting for my husband to come home. Then, when he got there, tiptoeing around him, waiting for him to go off. Because I knew it was only a matter of time until he hit me again."

"A matter of time," said the EeePavoosh.

"I remember." As Tillie stared off into space, drops of clear fluid ran out of her eyes and down her cheeks. "He beat me for bein' too pretty, 'cause other men were lookin' at me. He beat me so much, I wasn't pretty anymore." Reaching up, she lightly touched her face with her fingertips. "Then, he beat me for bein' too *ugly*.

"He beat me for gettin' pregnant, too...and then he beat me for losin' the baby." She wiped the fluid from her cheeks and rubbed her eyes hard. "As if I *wanted* to lose the only thing that had ever made me happy."

"And this made the time longer?" said the EeePavoosh.

"God, yes," said Tillie. "Each minute that he beat me lasted a century."

"Each minute lasted a century?" The EeePavoosh couldn't keep the excitement out of his voice.

Tillie nodded. "When it was over, and the bruises set in, the minutes lasted even longer. I'd be doin' the dishes or laundry, and my whole body would ache and sting from what he did, and the minutes would just crawl. I just wanted it all to be over…but the more I wanted that, the slower it went."

The EeePavoosh worked faster. If what Tillie was telling him was true, he couldn't wait to get to the other side of the portal.

"I know what you're thinkin'," said Tillie as she wiped away more fluid from her cheeks. "Why the hell did I stay with him for five years, right?"

The answer seemed perfectly clear to the EeePavoosh. "To continue to stretch out time. And consume it."

"Consume?" Tillie gave him a strange look. "What do you mean, 'consume' time?"

"Ingest it for sustenance," said the EeePavoosh. "Eat it."

The look on Tillie's face deepened. "Why do you say that?" She eased around to the other side of the portal and stared at him through the rippling oval.

"It is how I live," said the EeePavoosh. "I consume time."

"You actually eat it?" asked Tillie. "Hours, minutes, days, whatever?"

"As you understand time, that is correct," said the EeePavoosh.

"Ain't that somethin'?" Tillie gazed at him thoughtfully, pinching her lower lip between her thumb and forefinger. "So, uh…what happens if you open that doorway?"

"When, not if," said the EeePavoosh. "I have completed my analysis. I know how to open it now."

"That's wonderful. I can't wait to get home." Tillie kept staring and pinching her lower lip. "But what about you? What'll you do when the doorway opens?"

"Go through, of course." The EeePavoosh decoded an especially complex network of quantum filaments in the heart of the portal, beginning the process of unlocking it. "I will open the portal soon and go through."

"Then what?" asked Tillie. "Will you start eatin' up the time over there?"

"Yes," said the EeePavoosh. "But if short amounts of time can be stretched into long ones on the other side, my eating will not disrupt the timeline significantly. Minutes can last centuries, correct?"

Tillie pinched her lip harder. "That's true, but..."

"Then there will be plenty of time," said the EeePavoosh. "Now tell me more about how that works, how time stretches on the other side."

"All right then." Tillie frowned thoughtfully. "Let's see." She closed her eyes, then opened them again. "I toldja about the longest five years of my life. How 'bout the longest *month* of my life? How's that grab ya'?"

"Fine and dandy," said the EeePavoosh.

"So okay." Tillie cleared her throat. "So I finally decided to run away from Ray. I finally got up the gumption to get away from him. Basically took the clothes on my back and a little cash I'd been socking away and headed out on foot one night. Headed straight for the bus station." She smiled. "Let me tell you, it was the greatest feeling since I'd gotten away from my childhood home. The air was so sweet and cool. I was free, totally *free*." She slumped and shook her head. "At least till the drunk driving the pickup slammed into me."

"Drunk?" said the EeePavoosh as he unlocked another series of quantum filaments.

Tillie didn't bother explaining. "He did a hit-and-run and just left me there. It took hours for someone to find me. And then I ended up in the hospital for a month with guess who watchin' over me? *Ray*, that asshole."

"Asshole?" said the EeePavoosh.

"Yep." Tillie nodded grimly. "So there I am, layin' in that hospital bed with just about every bone in my body broken…and they're pumpin' me full of drugs, but there's still so much pain… and there's Ray, tellin' me what he's gonna do to me when I get healed and go home. How he's gonna make me suffer and pay for runnin' out on him."

"And this made the time longer?" said the EeePavoosh.

"Oh, yeah," said Tillie. "That month in the hospital was a year to me. *Ten* years."

"A month became ten years?"

"All I could do was lay there and pray I'd die before they sent me home." Tillie turned away from the portal and stared off into space. "The hours crawled…with the pain and Ray's awful voice and the casts and slings keepin' me trapped there. Every minute lasted forever."

The EeePavoosh felt a rush of excitement. "Every minute lasted *forever*?"

"Then, just before I was supposed to go home, a miracle happened. The nurse came and told me some joker'd killed Ray in a bar fight. I was *free* again." She turned back and smiled. "And that was when time started speeding up."

"Speeding up?" said the EeePavoosh.

"Didn't I mention that?" said Tillie. "Time speeds up sometimes on the other side."

The EeePavoosh suddenly became alarmed. "It does?"

Tillie narrowed her eyes and fixed her gaze on him. "You don't like that, do you? Is it because the time wouldn't be as good to eat?"

"Faster time is shorter time," said the EeePavoosh. "There is less of it to eat."

"You don't say." Tillie nodded thoughtfully. "Well, it happens a lot over there. And here's the thing." She pinched her lower lip.

"It might start out longer, but then it gets shorter all of a sudden. You just never know."

"It starts out longer?" said the EeePavoosh. "Then gets shorter?"

"That's right," said Tillie. "Like, for example…" She stared up at the sky, thinking, then looked back down at him. "When I found out earlier this year that I was terminal. I was drinkin' heavy and livin' on the street…and I started coughin' up blood. When I went to the free clinic, the doctor told me I had lung cancer, and it was gonna kill me in six months." Tillie sighed. "The hour I spent in the room with that doctor, when he told me all that, was probably the longest hour of my life."

"The longest hour?" Again, the EeePavoosh grew excited. In a flurry of subatomic space-time reengineering, he unlocked the biggest sequence of filaments yet.

Tillie shook her head slowly. "Maybe I shouldn't've cared after the shitty life I had…but I did. It still ripped my heart out." Droplets of clear fluid again trickled from the corners of her eyes and down her cheeks. "It was like I was trapped again. I wanted to run away, but all I could do was sit there and listen. And there was a clock in the office, an old-fashioned clock that ticked away the seconds…and it seemed like it took an *hour* between ticks."

"A second took an hour," said the EeePavoosh.

"That's right," said Tillie. "But ever since that hour, time's been goin' a million times faster. A *zillion*." She took a deep breath and let it out slowly. "Because it's runnin' out. And the closer I get to the end, the faster it goes."

A wave of disappointment rolled through the EeePavoosh. "Instead of getting longer, time is going faster?"

"You wouldn't *believe* how much faster," said Tillie.

The EeePavoosh thought it over, processing what she'd told him. How could time go faster? It was true that travel at relativistic speeds, those approaching the speed of light, could slow the passage of time for the traveler…but making it speed up was another matter.

Based on the stories Tillie had told, the flow of time must be very different on the other side…and not always in a good way. In some situations, it stretched out; in others, it shrank. How was that even possible?

And then there was an even more important question. "How do you control it? How do you make time longer or shorter?"

"I wish I knew," said Tillie. "I'd stretch out the time I've got left and make it last forever."

The EeePavoosh reached the last few quantum filaments keeping the portal shut. He was almost done with his work. "You eat time, too, then? You consume it as I do?"

"Time eats *me*, is more like it," said Tillie. "Every day, it wears me down a little more."

"And yet, the way you talk about time, you need it to survive."

Tillie nodded. "There's never enough."

"Then we both want the same thing."

"And I can't have it!" Tillie laughed bitterly. "You know what's funny? Most of my life, time dragged because things were so shitty. I just wanted it to speed up so the shittiness would end. But ever since I found out about the cancer, I just want it to slow down. I just want more of it."

On the verge of throwing the portal wide open, the EeeP-avoosh paused and gazed at Tillie through the rippling oval. More droplets ran down her cheeks; those droplets, and the way the breath was catching in her throat, had more to do with sadness than any kind of joy.

It was a sadness the EeePavoosh could identify with—the sadness of hunger. The sadness that came when there wasn't enough time to feed the ferocious craving that kept him alive.

Suddenly, a strange feeling took hold of him—a feeling of

alignment, of connection with a living being. How many life forms had died screaming when he'd gulped down their time-lines? And yet here he was, surging with affinity for one tiny creature from an alternate reality.

Here he was, an avatar of a light-years-long leviathan accustomed to straddling universes and devouring epochs, and he actually felt sympathy for one little anomalous female primate. Because just as she was running out of time, he'd been running out of it, too...with only one day left to devour in all the known feeding grounds.

At least until she'd shown him the portal and told him about the other side where time stretched out in ways he'd never imagined. Thanks to her, he stood on the threshold even now, ready to plunge into those rich new feeding grounds and gorge himself on the time they had to offer.

"I am ready to open the portal now," he announced.

"Wait a minute." Tillie scowled and pinched her lower lip. "Didn't you hear what I said about time speeding up? What if there isn't enough for you?"

"Hopefully, the stretched-out, longer time will make up for it," said the EeePavoosh.

"What'll be left when you're done?" said Tillie.

"When all time is devoured, nothing remains," said the EeePavoosh. "But if time can be made longer on the other side, there is nothing to worry about. If a little time can become a lot, the time-line will survive."

"That's true, that's true." Tillie shuffled her feet nervously. "But, uh, what if time doesn't work exactly the way you expect over there? If it runs the same as it does here, and it can't be made longer, you'll eat up all the time a lot sooner, right? The timeline won't survive."

"Theoretically," said the EeePavoosh.

"Then why take the chance?" said Tillie.

"Because I must feed. I must have more time in order to survive."

"Okay, listen." Tillie moved to stand between him and the portal. "Please don't do this. Don't go to the other side."

"I must," said the EeePavoosh. "I am hungry."

"So go somewhere else," said Tillie. "This is my home we're talkin' about here."

"There is nowhere else to go. Nowhere that I know of."

"Please," said Tillie. "For me. Don't do it."

"I must," said the EeePavoosh.

"Wait." Tillie threw her hands out in front of her. "Remember when I talked about my life meaning something? That maybe there's somethin' I'm supposed to do? What if this is it? Why I came here. To save my *world*."

"You should not care," said the EeePavoosh. "Your life was shitty."

"Not all of it, though," said Tillie. "There were good parts, I swear."

The EeePavoosh thought for a moment, gazing into her eyes. To ensure his survival, he could not do what she asked…yet the pull of his alignment with her was strong. The sympathy he felt for her demanded he do *something*.

Something, perhaps, that would repay the debt he owed her for leading him to the new feeding grounds. Something that would give her back the time she was running out of.

"Then tell me about one of the good parts," said the EeeP-avoosh. "If you could make one time of your life longer, which would it be?"

Tillie frowned. "Will that make you not go to the other side? Will that save my world?"

The EeePavoosh thrashed his tail. "Just answer the question, Tillie."

The air shimmered in a corner of the dimly lit hospital room. A rectangular outline appeared from floor to ceiling, traced in soft silver light…and then the space within the outline flashed, and Tillie stepped through.

She blinked hard, adjusting to the low light. Then, as the portal vanished behind her, her eyes went straight to the room's one bed. She couldn't see the occupants, because they were surrounded by a huddle of women with their backs turned to her…but she knew who they were. She knew exactly who was in that bed.

Instantly, a smile spread across her face. Tears ran from her eyes, and she didn't bother to wipe them away.

"Go ahead," said a soft voice from the shadows. "Go to them."

Turning, Tillie saw that the voice belonged to herself…another version of herself. And there were more besides, many more crowding around the room as well as huddling around the bed.

"Don't be afraid." One of them moved out of the shadows and took her arm. "There's nothing to be scared of anymore."

Tillie stared in wonder at her other self, the one holding her arm. The EeePavoosh had told her it would be like this, yet it was still so very strange seeing her mirror image staring back at her.

"This is your first time through the loop, isn't it?" said the other Tillie.

"Yes." Tillie nodded.

"We're all here for you." The other Tillie smiled and squeezed Tillie's arm. "We just keep coming, but there's always room for one more."

"Thank you." Tillie felt a welling-up of warmth, a deep, abiding comfort that she'd never felt before. Other hands touched her, reaching out from other selves, and she closed her eyes.

It was then she thought of the EeePavoosh. Where was he now? Off devouring the rest of the timeline, no doubt, bringing the end of time to the universe Tillie called home. She hadn't been able to stop him, back on the purple-and-yellow planet, or even delay him much. Her stories of stretched-out time, which she'd told to entice him to open the doorway, had made him want to cross over; by the time she'd realized her mistake and switched to stories of speeded-up time, it had been too late.

But it didn't matter anymore, did it? The EeePavoosh had been grateful and set aside this one hour for her, this hour forty years in her past which had now become her present and her future as well.

It was the first thing the EeePavoosh had done after coming through the portal. Tillie had told him about this one time in her life, this one good hour that she'd make longer if she could. Then he'd brought her back to it. He'd given it to her for helping him find the portal.

And she was going to spend the rest of her life here.

"Come on," said the other Tillie who was holding her arm. "You want to see this, don't you?"

Tillie opened her eyes. "Are you kiddin'?"

She shivered with anticipation as the other Tillie escorted her across the room. The women who were huddled around the hospital bed—Tillies, every one of them—slowly parted to make way for her.

Heart racing, tears flowing, she stepped forward. The last few Tillies moved aside, giving her the place of honor at the head of the bed.

"Hello," said the woman lying in the bed…the brown-haired twenty-year-old girl looking like an angel in her white hospital gown.

Her green-eyed gaze met Tillie's, and Tillie melted. Had she really been so beautiful forty years ago? Had she *ever* been so beautiful?

"Her name is Michelle." Young Tillie looked down at the newborn baby in her arms...so tiny and frail, she seemed to be fading into the little pink blanket in which she was wrapped.

The truth was, she really was fading. She had exactly one hour to live.

That one hour had been the happiest of Tillie's life. And it would be again, and again, until she faded out, too. Until the cancer took her.

Because the EeePavoosh had created a loop. At the end of the hour, after Michelle died, Tillie would go back to the start and live through it again. Every hour that remained before Tillie's own death, she would spend it here, stringing together a lifetime out of this repeated hour like a strand of glittering pearls.

Each time she started the loop again, she coexisted with past and future versions of herself who'd also entered it. All the Tillies from all the hours she had left to live were sharing that precious fragment of time and space...but somehow, the hospital room didn't seem crowded. They were all in this together; even the twenty-year-old version, to whom this experience rightfully belonged, didn't seem to mind the company.

"Would you like to hold her?" asked young Tillie.

"Yes, please." Tillie nodded and reached out.

When the tiny bundle touched her hands, it was like a bright new star blazed to life in her heart. It didn't matter who the baby's father was or how much pain he'd caused; it didn't matter why the child was sick or that she had less than an hour to live.

All that mattered was that this was *Tillie's* baby, her precious lost Michelle miraculously restored to her. And they would never be apart again for as long as they both lived.

Dozens of Tillies crowded around, beaming and cooing, but

the moment belonged only to those two at the head of the bed...
only mother and child, brought together after an eternity apart.

The baby squirmed, and Tillie trembled. Cradling Michelle in
her arms, she bent down and kissed her softly on the forehead.

And Michelle, as sickly as she was, as fast as she was fading,
opened her tiny green eyes and looked up at her. Their gazes met
for the first time in forever.

And they both smiled.

SAVAGE BREASTS

NINA KIRIKI HOFFMAN

I have been a fan of Nina Kiriki Hoffman's fiction since the day we chal-
lenged each other back when we were first starting out as young writers.

This story had become legend by the time Kris bought it for Pulphouse: The Hardback Magazine *back in the late 1980s. Nina had read*
it aloud at a few conventions, never being able to keep a straight face,
which caused the audience to react and it went from there. (Nina has an
infectious giggle so that when she laughs, it is impossible to not laugh
with her.)

Nina has written hundreds and hundreds of wonderful short stories
over the decades as well as many highly acclaimed fantasy and young
adult novels. You can't go wrong when picking up a Nina Kiriki
Hoffman story or novel.

———

I was only a lonely leftover on the table of Life. No one seemed
interested in sampling me.

I was alone that day in the company cafeteria when I made
the fateful decision which changed my life. If Gladys, the other
secretary in my boss's office and my usual lunch companion, had
been there, it might never have happened, but she had a dentist
appointment. Alone with the day's entree, Spaghetti-O's, I sought
company in a comic book I found on the table.

In the first blazing burst of inspiration I ever experienced, I
cut out an ad on the back of the *Wonder Woman* comic book. "The
Insult that Made a Woman Out of Wilma," it read. It showed a
hipless, flat-chested girl being buried in the sand and abandoned
by her date, who left her alone with the crabs as he followed a
bosomy blonde off the page. Wilma eventually excavated herself,
went home, kicked a chair, and sent away for Charlotte Atlas's
pamphlet, "From Beanpole to Buxom in 20 days or your money
back." Wilma read the pamphlet and developed breasts the size

of breadboxes. She retrieved her boyfriend and rendered him acutely jealous by picking up a few hundred other men.

I emulated Wilma's example and sent away for the pamphlet and the equipment that came with it.

When my pamphlet and my powder-pink exerciser arrived, I felt a vague sense of unease. Some of the ink in the pamphlet was blurry. A few pages were repeated. Others were missing. Sensing that my uncharacteristic spurt of enthusiasm would dry up if I took the time to send for a replacement, I plunged into the exercises in the book (those I could decipher) and performed them faithfully for the requisite twenty days. My breasts blossomed. Men on the streets whistled. Guys at the office looked up when I jiggled past.

I felt like a palm tree hand-pollinated for the first time. I began to have clusters of dates. I was pawed, pleasured, and played with. I experienced lots of stuff I had only read about before, and I mostly loved it after the first few times. The desert I'd spent my life in vanished; everything I touched here in the center of the mirage seemed real, intense, throbbing with life. I exercised harder, hoping to make the reality realler.

Then parts of me began to fight back.

I reclined on Maxwell's couch, my hands behind my head, as he unbuttoned my shirt, unhooked my new, enormous, front-hook bra, and opened both wide. He kissed my stomach. He feathered kisses up my body. Suddenly my left breast flexed and punched him in the face. He was surprised. He looked at me suspiciously. I was surprised myself. I studied my left breast. It lay there gently bobbing like a Japanese glass float on a quiet sea. Innocent. Waiting.

Maxwell stared at my face. Then he shook his head. He eyed my breasts. Slowly he leaned closer. His lips drew back in a pucker. I waited, tingling, for them to flutter on my abdomen again. No such luck. Both breasts surged up and gave him a double whammy.

It took me an hour to wake him up. Once I got him conscious, he told me to get out! Out! And take my unnatural equipment with me. I collected my purse and coat and, with a last look at him as he lay there on the floor by the couch, I left.

In the elevator my breasts punched a man who was smoking a cigar. He coughed, choked, and called me unladylike. A woman told me I had done the right thing.

When I got home I took off my clothes and looked at myself in the mirror. What beautiful breasts. Pendulous. Centerfold quality. Heavy as water balloons. Firm as paperweights. I would be sorry to say goodbye to them. I sighed, and they bobbled. "Well, guys, no more exercise for you," I said. I would have to let them go. I couldn't let my breasts become a Menace to Mankind. I would rather be noble and suffer a bunch.

I took a shower and went to bed.

That night I had wild dreams. Something was chasing me, and I was chasing something else. I thought maybe I was chasing myself, and that scared me silly. I kept trying to wake up, but to no avail. When I finally woke, exhausted and sweaty, in the morning, I discovered my sheets twisted around my legs. My powder-pink exerciser lay beside me in the bed. My upper arms ached the way they did after a good workout.

At work, my breasts interfered with my typing. The minute I looked away from my typewriter keyboard to glance at my steno pad, my breasts pushed between my hands, monopolized the keys, and drove my Selectric to distraction. After an hour of trying to cope with this I told my boss I had a sick headache. He didn't want me to go home. "Mae June, you're quite an ornament to the office these days," he said. "Can't you just sit out there and look pretty and suffering? More and more of my clients have remarked on how you spruce up the decor. If that clackety-clacking bothers your pretty little head, why, I'll get Gladys to take your work and hers and type in the closet."

"Thank you, sir," I said. I went back out in the front room and sat far away from everything my breasts could knock over. Gladys sent me vicious looks as she flat-chestedly crouched over her early-model IBM and worked twice as hard as usual.

For a while I was happy just to rest. After all that nocturnal exertion, I was tired. My chair wasn't comfortable, but my body didn't care. Then I started feeling rotten. I watched Gladys. She had scruffy hair that kept falling out of its bobby pins and into her face. She kept her fingernails short and unpolished and she didn't seem to care how carelessly she chose her clothes. She reminded me of the way I had looked two months earlier, before men started getting interested in me and giving me advice on what to wear and what to do with my hair. Gladys and I no longer went to lunch together. These days I usually took the boss's clients to lunch.

"Why don't you tell the boss you have a sick headache too?" I asked. "There's nothing here that can't wait 'til tomorrow."

"He'd fire me, you fool. I can't waggle my femininity in his face like you can. Mae June, you're a cheater."

"I didn't mean to cheat," I said. "I can't help it." I looked at her face to see if she remembered how we used to talk at lunch. "Watch this, Gladys." I turned back to my typewriter and pulled off the cover. The instant I inserted paper, my breasts reached up and parked on the typewriter keys. I leaned back, straightening up, then tried to type the date in the upper right-hand corner of the page. Plomp plomp. No dice. I looked at Gladys. She had that kind of look that says *eyoo, ick, that's creepy, show it to me again*.

I opened my mouth to explain about Wilma's insult and Charlotte Atlas when my breasts firmed up. I found myself leaning back to display me at an advantage. One of the boss's clients had walked in.

"Mae June, my nymphlet," said this guy, Burl Weaver. I had been to lunch with him before. I kind of liked him.

Gladys touched the intercom. "Sir, Mr. Weaver is here."

"Aw, Gladys," said Burl, one of the few men who had learned her name as well as mine, "why'd you haveta spoil it? I didn't come here for business."

"Burl?" the boss asked over the intercom. "What does he want?"

Burl strode over to my desk and pushed my transmit button. "I'd like to borrow your secretary for the afternoon, Otis. Any objections?"

"Why no, Burl, none at all." Burl is one of our biggest accounts. We produce the plastic for the records his company produces. "Mae June, you be good to Burl now."

Burl pressed my transmit button for me. I leaned as near to my speaker as I could get. "Yes, sir," I said. With tons of trepidation, I rose to my feet. My previous acquaintance with Burl had gone further than my acquaintance with Maxwell yesterday. Now that my breasts were seceding from my body, how could I be sure I'd be nice to Burl? What if I lost the company our biggest account?

With my breasts thrust out before me like dogs hot on a scent, I followed Burl out of the office, giving Gladys a misery-laden glance as I closed the door behind me. She gave me a suffering nod in return. At least there was somebody on my side, I thought, as Burl and I got on the elevator. I tried to cross my arms over my breasts but they pushed my arms away. A familiar feeling of helplessness, one I knew well from before I sent away for that pamphlet, washed over me. Except this time I didn't feel my fate lay on the knees of the gods. No. My life was in the hands of my breasts, and they seemed determined to throw it away.

Burl waited until the elevator got midway between floors, then hit the stop button. "Just think, Mae June, here we are, suspended in midair," he said. "Think we can hump hard enough to make this thing drop? Wanna try? Think we'll even notice when she hits bottom?" With each sentence he got closer to me, until at last he was pulling the zip down the back of my dress.

I smiled at Burl and wondered what would happen next. I felt like an interested spectator at a sports event. Burl pulled my dress down around my waist.

"You sure look nice today, Mae June, " he said, staring at my front, then at my lips. My breasts bobbled obligingly, and he looked down at them again. "Like you got little joy machines inside," he said, gently unhooking my bra.

Joy buzzers, I thought. Jolt city.

"You like me, don't you, Mae June? I can be real nice." He stroked me.

"Sure I like you, Burl."

"Would you like to work for me? I sure like you, Mae June. I'd like to put you in a nice little apartment on the top story of a real tall building with an elevator in it." As he talked, he kneaded at me like a kitten. "An express elevator. It would only stop at your floor and the basement. We could lock it from the inside. We could ride it. Up. Down. Up. Down. Hell, we could put a double bed in it. You'd like that, wouldn't you, Mae June?"

"Yes, Burl." When would my mammaries make their move?

He bent his head forward to pull down his own zipper, and they conked him. "Wha?" he said as he recoiled and collapsed gracefully to the floor. "How the heck did you do that, Mae June?"

I decided Burl had a harder head than Maxwell.

"Your hands are all snarled up in your dress. You been taking aikido or something?"

"No, Burl."

"Jeepers, if you didn't like me, you shoulda said something. I woulda left you alone."

"But I do like you, Burl. It's my breasts. They make their own decisions."

He lay on the floor and looked up at me. 'That's the dumbest-assed thing I ever heard," he said. He rolled over and got to his feet. Then he came over, leaned toward me, and glared at my breasts. The left one flexed. He jumped back just in time. "Mae June, are you possessed?"

"Yes!" That must be it. The devil was in my breasts. I wondered what I had done to deserve such a fate. I wasn't even religious.

Burl made the sign of the cross over my breasts. Nothing happened. "That's not it," he said. "Maybe it's your subconscious. You hate men. Something like that. So how come this didn't happen last time, huh?" He began pacing.

"They were waiting to get strong enough. Oh, Burl, what am I going to do?"

"Get dressed. I think you better see a doctor, Mae June. Maybe we can get 'em tranquilized or something. I don't like the way they're sitting there, watching me."

I managed to hook my bra without too much trouble. Burl zipped me up and turned the elevator operational again. "Do you hate me?" I asked him on the way down.

"Course I don't hate you," he said, shifting a step away from me. "You're real pretty, Mae June. Just as soon as you get yourself under control, you're gonna make somebody a real nice little something. I just don't want to take too many chances. Suppose what you've got is contagious? Suppose some of my body parts decide they don't like women? Let's be rational about this, huh?"

"I mean—you won't drop the contract with IPP, will you?"

"Shoot no. You worried about job security? I like that in a woman. You got sense. I won't complain. But I hope you got Blue Cross. You may have to get those knockers psychoanalyzed or something."

He offered to drive me to a doctor or the hospital. I told him I'd take the bus. He tried to get me to change my mind. He failed. I watched him drive away. Then I went home.

I picked up the powder-pink exerciser and took it to the window. My apartment was on the tenth floor. I was just going to drop the exerciser out the window when I looked down and saw Gladys's red coat wrapped around Gladys. My doorbell rang. I buzzed her into the building.

By the time she arrived at my front door I had collapsed on the couch, still holding the exerciser. "It's open," I called when she knocked. My arms were pumping the exerciser as I lay there. I thought about trying to stop exercising, but decided it was too much effort. "How'd you know I'd be home?" I asked Gladys as she came in and took off her coat.

"Burl stopped by the office."

"Did he say what happened?"

"No. He said he was worried about you. What did happen?"

They punched him." I pumped the exerciser harder. "What am I going to do? I can't type, and now I can't even do lunch." I glared at my breasts. "You want us to starve?"

They were doing push-ups and didn't answer.

Gladys sat on a chair across from me and leaned forward, her gaze fixed on my new features. Her mouth was open.

My arms stopped pumping without me having anything to say about it. My left arm handed the exerciser to her. Her gaze still locked on my breasts, Gladys gripped the powder-pink exerciser and went to work.

"Don't," I said, sitting up. Startled, she fell against the chair back. "Do you want this to happen to you?"

"I—I—" She gulped and dropped the exerciser.

"I don't know what they want!" I stared at them with loathing. "It won't be long before the boss realizes I'm not an asset. Then what am I going to do?"

"You...you have a lot of career choices," said Gladys. "Like— have you ever considered mud wrestling?"

"What?"

"Exotic dancing?" She blinked. She licked her upper lip. "You could join the FBI, I bet. 'My breasts punched out spies for God and country.' You could sell your story to the *Enquirer*. 'Double-breasted Death.' Sounds like a slick detective movie from the Thirties. You could—"

"Stop," I said, "I don't want to hear any more."

"I'm sorry," she said after a minute. She got up and made tea.

We were sitting there sipping it when she had another brain-storm. "What do they want? You've been asking that yourself. What are breasts for, anyway?"

"Sex and babies," I said.

We looked at each other. We looked away. All those lunches, and we had never talked about it. I bet she only knew what she read in books too.

She stared at the braided rug on the floor. "Were you...protected?"

I stared at the floor too. "I don't think so."

"They have tests you can do at home."

———

I thought it was Burl's, so my breasts and I went to visit him. "You talk to them," I said. "If they think you're the father, maybe they won't beat you up anymore. Maybe they're just fending off all other comers."

Between the three of them they reached an arrangement. I moved into that penthouse apartment.

I shudder to think what they'll do when the baby comes.

FICTION

JERRY OLTION

Without equal, Jerry Oltion is the most prolific writer of short stories in the history of Analog Magazine. *And new stories still appear there regularly.*

These days, besides continuing his regular science fiction writing, Jerry is also a major amateur astronomer and does a regular column for Sky and Telescope.

This story takes on an old idea about writers, twists it into a comment on the publishing industry, and then makes it completely wonderful in very few words, something only a master like Jerry could do.

————

Roger knew the doctors were approaching by the squeak of their soft-soled shoes on the waxed floor. Damn. Just when he was getting to the good part. He read faster, hoping he could at least make it to a scene break before they interrupted him.

They discussed him as they approached, as if he weren't there. Roger was getting used to that. He tried to tune them out and concentrate on the perils of Laura Morrison, who was putting on her spacesuit, not knowing the fabric under the arms had weakened with age.

The new one, no doubt a fresh intern, had a penetrating voice. "Why does he hold his arms out like that?" he asked. "Does he think he's driving?"

"No," said the regular doctor, Williams. "He says he's reading."

"Breeding? He thinks there's a woman—"

"No, no. *Reading.* He claims he's holding onto a bunch of thin sheets of wood all bound together on one edge, and he's looking at some sort of marks on them."

Teigh and Laura stood in the airlock while the pressure dropped to zero. Laura's suit bulged with the strain, but held.

"How strange. Is he responsive?"

Doctor Williams snorted. "Barely. He's usually quite reluctant to give up his delusion. Let me show you. Roger?"

Teigh led Laura out of the airlock, and Laura, seeing the stars for the first time in decades, leaned her head back and said, "Hah, hasn't changed much."

"Roger."

"Do his eyes always flick from side to side like that?"

"Only when he's 'reading.' Roger, this is Doctor Gordon. Can you say hello to him for me?"

They climbed into the rocket car for the five-minute journey to the starship under construction. Laura's suit creaked ominously as she stretched to reach the seatbelt.

"Roger."

Roger sighed and lowered the book. Doctor Williams and the intern (his name already forgotten) stood before him, their white lab coats spotless, their faces contorted in artificial smiles. Roger said, "Could you maybe come back in a few minutes? I've just got a couple of pages to go, and—"

"Pages?" the intern asked, ignoring Roger's request.

"Pages." Roger rattled the one he'd been reading. His eyes caught the line, *...drowned out in the hiss of escaping air...*and he knew he'd been right. Her suit hadn't held.

"And what do you see on those...pages?"

Roger sighed. "I see a great story about an old woman who lives on a space colony. Right now she's outside for the first time in years, and her spacesuit is about to blow. Now if you wouldn't mind, I'd like to—"

"He seems quite coherent, other than the obvious delusion," the intern remarked.

Doctor Williams sniffed. "Oh yes. But I'm nearly convinced that this 'reading' of his, these imaginary 'books' he examines, are symptoms of a much deeper disturbance. For instance, many of the stories he describes to me, supposedly from the pages of these books, involve murder and death. Others show an obsession with sex. They nearly always concern people in dire circumstances."

"Blowout!" Teigh shouted into the radio. "I've got someone with a suit blowout! Help me!"

"Do they indeed? How intriguing."

The shoes squeaked as the two doctors walked away. Doctor Williams said, "When you've got the time, you should have him read aloud to you. It's incredible. He can go on for hours without repeating himself, spinning new fantasies as fast as he can talk."

Teigh watched helplessly while the medics forced air into her lungs...

"Astounding."

"Oh, indeed. It's one of the most elaborate delusional systems I've ever encountered. He's not only come up with a whole new —though admittedly farfetched—method of information transfer, but he imagines a whole industry established to support it."

"Does he now?"

At last Laura was breathing on her own; horrible, bubbling breaths that made Teigh sick to listen to, but she was alive again.

"He described it to me once. The mechanics of it alone are incredibly complex. But what I'd like to know," Doctor Williams said as they rounded the corner at the far end of the hall, "is where he gets all those *ideas*."

GROUP

RAY VUKCEVICH

This story by Ray Vukcevich has stuck with me since the first time I read it and bought it over twenty-five years ago. There is just something haunting and creepy and all too true about it.

Ray's mind doesn't see story or fiction like any other writer and his stories right from the start have always fit Pulphouse. *I am honored to bring this one forward in time for a brand new set of readers. It just felt perfect for this first issue.*

————

Henry Popovich comes onstage holding a ten dollar bill in his left hand the way he might hold up a torch—low enough to look casual but high enough so the flames won't catch his hair. A pale white hand swoops out of the gloom, snatches his money, slaps a Mr. Microphone (tm) into his palm, and disappears again.

The cordless microphone always reminds Henry of his penis. Not that his penis is so long and hard, not that the head of his penis is so bulbous and black, not that his shaft is so smooth and white as the ivory plastic of his Mr. Microphone. He has no little black on/off switch on his penis. None of that. Still he thinks of his penis every time the disembodied hand exchanges his money for the long, cool Mr. Microphone. Henry holds it in front of his pants now and waggles it up and down, hoping Mary will loom up like a ship in the fog and say, "That's disgusting, Henry."

That never happens. Henry raises the plastic microphone to his lips and gets down to business. He thumbs on the little black switch and says, "Mary? Mary? Come in, Mary."

The dark stage stretches for miles in every direction. Henry can see scattered fires in oil drums glowing softly in the fog like lighthouses on a ragged coastline. Three levels of traffic crisscross above, rumbling steadily like a monstrous waterfall. The fog smells of gasoline and stiff winter weeds and shattered, frozen beer bottles, asphalt and cardboard popcorn boxes.

All around him, people bundled in their winter coats and scarfs and hats shuffle in and out of the fog and shadows, paths crossing and crossing again. Everyone has a Mr. Microphone; everyone calls.

"Donald? Donald? Come in, Donald."

"Greta. Can you hear me, Greta?"

"Come in, Sammy. Sammy, come in!"

"Are you there, Lisa? Lisa?"

"Walter? Walter? Come in, Walter."

Henry's daughter, Jennifer, her blond pigtails flying, runs across the stage, yelling into her microphone, "Mommy? Mommy? Come in, Mommy." A moment later she runs back the other way. "Daddy? Daddy? Come in, Daddy."

A spotlight dazzles Henry, freezing him in place. He groans. Spotlighted as he is, he must soliloquize. He's sure no one ever listens to his speeches. Beyond his spotlight's wavering circle of smoky light, the people still move and mull and murmur into their microphones.

"Hello? Hello?" He taps the bulb of his microphone. "I'm Henry Popovich. I'm 44, and as you can see I've gone bald. Just this year. I wish my wife could understand how that makes me feel. Just overnight I look like my father. Well, I don't mean to sound pathetic, but I'd just like to say that when I look in the mirror, I sometimes don't know who I am. I'm a stranger. You're all strangers, too. I'm sure you're all nice people, but I don't know you. It can get pretty lonely. Well, whatever. I'd just like to say what a comfort it is to be here. Any chance at all of getting through, you know, of being heard, is better than none at all. Well, I guess. . ."

The spotlight snaps off, and Henry stands in darkness again. He sighs and raises his microphone. "Mary? Mary? Come in, Mary."

Downstage the spotlight comes on again. Mary speaks. No one listens.

"I'm Mary Popovich," she says. "I paint. My husband doesn't notice or maybe he thinks it's cute. I'll bet he thinks my real work is Jennifer and the house. Sure paint if you have time. Why not? No one will tell me if what I do is any good or not. Why won't someone talk to me?" The spotlight moves on, leaving her in the dark.

The spotlight sweeps around the stage looking for another speaker. It catches Jennifer.

"I don't have anything to say!" Jennifer runs screaming, and the spotlight follows her like a garden hose tormenting a spider.

Someone bumps into Henry from the back, and he turns to deliver a severe look. Mary stands before him, her microphone raised to her lips, her long brown hair damp from the fog and pasted to her head. Her eyes go wide, and she takes a step back. Before he can seize the moment, he takes a step back, too. The fog between them blurs her face. He knows this is his big chance. He hopes he hasn't blown it.

"I'm bald!" he yells.

Someone wanders between them. Henry takes another step back and loses Mary in the fog.

Jennifer circles screaming, "Mommy? Daddy? Come in, someone. Help! Help!" She can't get away from the spotlight.

"Mary? Mary? Come in, Mary," Henry says.

"Henry? Henry? Come in, Henry." Mary's voice fades and is gone.

————

Better luck another time. Henry decides to call it a night. He's given it his best shot. He turns and walks toward the exit. Jennifer runs after him still screaming for him to come in. The spotlight won't leave her alone until she makes a little speech, discusses her feelings. She knows that, and just as Henry reaches the exit, she stops running, stops screaming, raises her Mr. Microphone and says, "Muffy died. My dog. I feel so alone. I hope you're satisfied." She kicks at the stage. "Muffy? Muffy? Come in, Muffy."

Tonight that is apparently enough. The light leaves her and sweeps across the stage to catch a woman with orange hair. The woman freezes like a deer befuddled by automobile headlights. Then she pulls herself together and speaks.

Henry doesn't listen. He steps through the exit. He turns in his Mr. Microphone and slumps down on a bench to wait for his family. Jennifer comes out and stands quietly by his side, keeping her hands to herself. A few moments later, Mary comes out, and the three of them walk home. Jennifer walks between them, her arms stiff at her sides like she's pretending to be an animated corpse. Mary's got her arms folded under her breasts. Henry walks with his hands in his pockets. Not another peep is heard from any of them.

LOOKING FOR THE BASTARD

DAVID H. HENDRICKSON

David H. Hendrickson might be one of the most diverse writers I have had the pleasure to meet. His sports novels, Cracking the Ice *(about hockey) and* Offensive Foul *(that takes on basketball), are considered two of the best sports books in recent memory. And he also just published a book for writers on how to get books into schools.*

He is also a major nonfiction writer, with over fifteen hundred works of non-fiction. And then there are his diverse short stories that range from a story called "Tiffany Gets Her Boobs" to stories in Ellery Queen *magazine to this gut-twisting story below.*

"Looking for the Bastard" is an original story to this magazine and it twists me up every time I look at it.

———

I'm standing on the platform. Alone. Looking for the bastard.

Walked up the twenty-one cracked and crumbling concrete steps to get here from the deserted street below, leaning hard on the rusted, black handrail.

Don't see nothing, other than the usual: crushed out cigarette butts, white-splattered pigeon droppings, a crumpled bag from McDonald's, and a used condom over near the graffiti-filled cement wall.

The place smells of urine. Maybe my own sweat, too. It was hot today, almost ninety and humid. I ain't had a good, hot shower in a while. Ain't had a good meal in a while, neither.

But I pay that no mind.

Cause I'm looking for the bastard.

Looking for him through a darkness broken only by the haunting glow cast by the floodlights spaced fifty feet apart, humming their high-pitched tune above my mostly bald, black head. Further off down the platform, at the end where the flood-lights can't quite penetrate the darkness and the weeds poke out of the concrete cracks, rats squeal.

My tired bones creak as I move my scrawny ass in little more than a shuffle toward the dark gray trash bin of my nightmares. Overflowing, it's chained to one of the puke green pillars that rise to the metal overhang above, an overhang that sounds like drum beats when it rains. The trash bin smells of its garbage, not quite ripe but still garbage. I poke about, but see nothing.

I scratch the gray whiskers on my face and move closer to the tracks. I look across to the red brick three-story factory building a couple hundred feet away, but no lights are on. I look down at the tracks to make sure the bastard ain't down there, the toes of my scuffed and tattered brown shoes on the three-inch-wide, yellow caution line. But he ain't there.

Caution.

Now that's a word for ya.

————

Some who don't understand what it's like for people like us say we shouldn't ever play the lottery. Should spend that money on food and rent and clothes and shoes for our feet. They may have a point, but they don't know what its like to have no hope, to be like a drowning man whose head finally pokes above water, but before he even gets a chance to gulp so much as a single breath of air, a large wave or a strong, hateful hand slams him back under.

That's what I felt like back before everything changed. On the wait list for a place in the projects cause we couldn't afford the rent. A trip to the grocery store didn't never get no cheaper. And little Angie, our only child, a sweet nine-year-old girl who wouldn't hurt a fly, seemed to outgrow her clothes fast as we could buy them, and not just cause she was chubby. And when she needed the medicine, it was like taking my whole paycheck and flushing it down the toilet.

Ain't like we was spending our money on trips to A-ruba.

So every now and then, I'd spend a dollar I shouldn'ta spent on a lottery ticket. I knew I shouldn't, but I couldn't help myself. I just needed a little bit of hope, you know?

Hope that I'd actually bust out of that overwhelming wave and actually get to breathe.

And you know what? The most blessed miracle ever came down from Heaven above.

Or so I thought.

I won! Over six hundred and fifty thousand dollars!

Six hundred and fifty...*thousand*...dollars.

Course I coulda taken it in something they called an annuity where they'd pay me a little each year, but a man like me whose been lied to and cheated what feels like every day of his life ain't taking no annuity.

Give me the cash money and let me breathe, man, let me breathe!

I tell you, there was a lot of tears in our kitchen the night I brought home that check and showed it to my wife, Gerty—a thin, tired-looking woman with an almost constant look of sadness in her eyes—and then to Angie. Gerty certainly didn't look tired anymore and that look of sadness in her eyes was gone. I don't know if I ever seen her happier, except the day Angie was born. We was all crying and laughing and jumping up and down for joy.

Specially Angie. Her mother, and other busybodies who can't seem to mind their own business, would tell her not to be so loud all the time. Shush, girl. Tone it down. You embarrassing.

But her mother wasn't telling Angie to tone it down that night even as that little butterball of sweetness whooped it up as loud as a jet airplane taking off.

Whoo-ee. Our joy was complete.

I was half a mind to go down to the plant and tell the super— a white man named Joe Gordon who'd walk over his momma and grandma, too, just to get ahead, and who hadn't minded walking all over the likes of me—that he could take his goddamned job and stick it somewhere.

But I ain't stupid.

Six hundred and fifty thousand dollars is a lot of money, a whole lot more than just a life preserver tossed to this drowning man, but not enough to live on for the rest of your life. Not even if you're single, much less a man with a wife and a nine-year-old girl.

So I wasn't going to be a fool and quit my job or be a real damned fool and punch that Joe Gordon right in the nose, like he deserved. I was still gonna show up each day, put in my time, and keep collecting that paycheck.

I might have a whole different goddamned attitude, I'll tell you that. A *whole* different goddamned attitude. But I wasn't gonna get myself fired or nothing stupid like that. I was gonna mind my business and take care of business.

And that's exactly what I did.

Didn't even let that damned Joe Gordon know I won six hundred and fifty thousand dollars, though he found out—word gets around about that sort of thing—and he kinda looked at me different for a while there, as if he was expecting me to punch him in the mouth like he deserved.

But I was smart. I was finally able to breathe the air about me. And even if it wasn't no sweet mountain air or no rich Beverly Hills air with the smell of chlorine in the pools and rose bushes and bark mulch in the flower bed, it was air.

Gritty, dirty city air, but air.

I could breathe.

Until Angie disappeared and the bastard left his ransom note in our mail slot.

Hey Rich Man,

If you ever want to see your little girl again, be near your phone at 7:30 tonight for the next directions.

NO COPS! If I even think *I see one of them, I'll cut your little girl open like a plump Thanksgiving Day turkey.*

———

Took a long time to get the six hundred thousand in cash. Not the full six hundred and fifty thousand. The bastard, his voice coarse and distorted over the phone, had laughed and said he assumed I'd spent fifty grand already, a fool like me always does that, and if I hadn't, wasn't he a nice guy leaving me all that dough?

So I bought me a briefcase, a cheap one, dark brown with no lock—never had reason to own a briefcase before that—and I packed all that money in it. Had Gerty drive me to the train station. We didn't say nothing. Didn't look at each other.

Didn't have to.

Couldn't.

Just sat in the darkness of the car down below the station, parked along the curbside, and waited, looking up at it every few seconds, our hearts pounding even while they were breaking. Sweat formed on our foreheads, the air heavy and warm. My fists clenched and unclenched. Beside me, Gerty softly sobbed.

The 9:58 p.m. train arrived in a whoosh of air, noisy and screeching. What felt like several lifetimes later, it left. Several lifetimes after that, a couple emerged from the concrete stairwell and walked the couple hundred yards down the street to the commuter parking lot.

Several lifetimes after that, I walked up the twenty-one stairs alone, the briefcase in one hand and the plastic bag of trash I'd brought, following the bastard's directions, in the other. They felt like they weighed a couple hundred tons, but that was nothing compared to how heavy my heart felt.

Not because I cared about the money.

Oh, I cared about the money, all right. There was six hundred *thousand* dollars inside that briefcase, after all. That money had let me breathe, given me hope for our family's future.

Angie's future. She could get her crooked teeth fixed. She could go to college. Be something more than her father, just a poor, dumb laborer at the plant who got lucky with a couple numbers on a ticket.

She could be anything.

But it was turning out that money wasn't going to let me breathe. Wasn't going to let my little girl get her teeth fixed or go to college and make something out of herself. This drowning man had gotten his couple gulps of air, but now a hateful, cruel hand was thrusting me down beneath the waves one last time, this one for good.

So much for luck.

All I wanted now was to get my little girl back. To hell with the goddamned money, just so long as I got Angie back. So I'd said nothing to the police. Didn't trust them to protect my little girl. I'd seen too many things in my lifetime to trust them at all.

So I was on my own. Nobody but me up here and Gerty down in the car.

I was alone here on the platform, but the bastard had to be here or nearby somewhere. Had to be watching me somehow, perhaps from a window in the old, red brick, three-story factory building on the other side of the tracks set back a few hundred feet. No lights shone in any of the windows, but I knew the bastard had to be in there somewhere.

Watching me go to the chained trash bin, now only half filled with trash. Place the loaded suitcase into the trash bin and cover it with the plastic bag of my own trash.

I looked over at the factory building and pointed to the trash bin, sure he was watching. I touched a hand to my heart, and clasped my hands in a begging gesture.

Then I went back down to the car, nodded quick to Gerty who looked away and broke into gasping sobs even as tears streaked down my own face.

And we waited for first the 10:14 train, and then the 10:43 to arrive.

The 10:43. The train that was supposed to have Angie aboard. Making no sense at all, I thought of how that was after her bedtime. As if that mattered at all now.

We were told to stay away until that train arrived and we did. No one entered or left the station for the 10:14, and no one came to wait for the 10:43.

As soon as we heard the train rumbling down the tracks and clanging to announce its arrival, we bolted from the car, not locking it, not even thinking to slam shut the doors. We shot up those twenty-one stairs, ignoring the black handrail, and were there waiting long before the train came to a screeching halt.

Of course, Angie didn't step off that train and run crying into our arms.

Of course, the suitcase full of money was gone, the plastic bag of trash left behind.

And of course, of course, of course, Angie's lifeless body was found days later in a dumpster behind a Burger King.

In a goddamned dumpster. My little girl.

———

We was on the TV news for two days. Mostly about how what fools we'd been not to trust the police, or the FBI if it had come to that, to get our Angie back. The TV reporters shook their heads at our stupidity, and how now the odds were stacked against finding the killer. And on one station, a newscaster raised an eyebrow at what a man like me was doing buying a lottery ticket in the first place.

Then the world forgot us.

For us, it was almost a blessing, but I couldn't help thinking about JonBenet whatshername with her pretty face, curly blonde hair, and beauty pageant smile. She got kidnapped and killed just like Angie—unless her parents killed her, of course—but while everyone has forgotten about Angie, JonBenet whatshername lives on in TV movies and shows, twenty, twenty-five years after her death.

I know why ain't no one gonna do a TV movie about Angie. She wasn't a cute, white girl with pretty blonde hair. Angie was a big, black girl, and the TV don't like big, black girls unless they on daytime TV shows about cheating boyfriends and paternity tests, and even then the TV just making fun of those girls. Any fool knows that. No, my Angie wasn't gonna be in no beauty pageants like that JonBenet whatshername.

But the TV oughta remember my girl cause her laughter, even if it was too loud, could warm a house with no heat in the dead of winter. She had a sweetness I bet that JonBenet couldn't hold a candle to.

And that bastard snuffed that laughter and sweetness out.

All because of that damned six hundred and fifty thousand dollars. The day doesn't go by that I don't regret buying that damned lottery ticket.

Maybe it isn't that big a deal that the world has forgotten about Angie. If it remembered her, that wouldn't bring her back. If it remembered her, that wouldn't bring my Gerty back either, Gerty who finally couldn't take it no more and swallowed the entire bottle of the sleeping pills her doctor had prescribed.

The bastard took it all away.

And so I'm alone. Whether it's at our empty apartment—*my*

empty apartment—or up on the elevated platform of that train station, I'm alone.

That's why I keep looking for the bastard who stole away my little girl. Who stole away my life. I figure he'll come back to the scene of his crime some day.

And I'll catch him. I don't know exactly what I'll do when that happens, but I sure have given it a lot of thought.

So every night when the 9:58 train is about to come rumbling and clanging into the station, I climb those twenty-one stairs, their concrete a little more cracked and crumbling each time, the black handrail a little more rusted.

It's been almost thirty years now that I've been coming here.

Thirty years. Every night.

Looking for the bastard.

SUBSCRIPTIONS

Don't Miss an Issue!
Subscribe

Electronic Subscription:
One Year... 4 Issues... $15.99

Paper Subscription:
One Year... 4 Issues... $29.99

For Full Subscription Information go to:
www.pulphousemagazine.com

All Issues Also Available at Your Favorite Bookstore

ACKNOWLEDGMENTS

Thank you to the following wonderful people who supported the 2017 *Pulphouse Fiction Magazine* Kickstarter Subscription Drive.

Steve Perry
Steve Jenkins
Valerie Brook
Woelf Dietrich
Christian Wood
Michael A. Burstein
Martin Greening
Lynette Aspey
Mary Jo Rabe
Nancy Sweetland
Denise Baker Gaskins
Jim Gotaas
Paula Meengs
Amy Browning
Anders M. Ytterdahl

Tasha Turner

Darragh Metzger

Tony

Dan 'Grimmund' Long

Wulf Moon

David Macpherson

Linda Banche

Lianne

M. L. Buchman

Ken Hattaway

Sharan Volin

Ryan M. Williams

Justin Burnett

Brian D Lambert

Thomas Bull

Andreas Flögel

Marianne Villanueva

Meyari McFarland

Amadan

Linda Bruno

Maralee Nelder

Jessica Doyle

Tony Hernandez

Pierre L'Allier

B.J. Baye

John Ordover

AJ Lemke

John Devenny

Debb & O'Neil De Noux

Doug Houseman

Vera Soroka

Chuck Gatlin

C Kobayashi

Cathy Green

Kate Pavelle

Leah

Willard A. Stone

Chuck Emerson

John Lorentz & Ruth Sachter

Paul McNamee

Eric Kent Edstrom

Stephanie Lucas

Keith Garrett

Keith Beals

Kristyn Willson

Dayle Dermatis

Risa Scranton

Piet Wenings

Mark Kuhn

Kathryn Goldman

David Macfarlane

Ron Vitale

Walter Hawn

David Bruns

Diana Deverell

Lois Malby Olmstead

Rob Menaul

Sean Mead

Mary Haldeman

AnnieB

Diane Sayer

Sam McDonald

Katherine Crispin

Skevos Mavros

Danny Evarts

Kai

Jaq Greenspon
Doug Red
Sara Litt
Simo Muinonen
Lisa Silverthorne
Kathryn Hodghead
Rick Lawler
Caryl Giles
Charles Pearson
C. Kirk
Darren Eggett
Lisa Owen
Blythe Ayne
Erik T Johnson
Kate MacLeod
Lillian Csernica
Ann Kellett
J Stuart Pratt
Sam Turner
D.V. Berkom
Greg Gorden
Jeff Metzner
Nancy Johnson
Robert Clemens
Joy Oestreicher
Christina
FredH
John Rogers
Donald Mark
Gary Piserchio
Richard Boulter
Anne J
Dawn Watson

Tanith Korravai

Cassidy Percoco

Marnilo C

Vito Michienzi

Jason Zippay

Terry gene, novelist

John M. Portley

Andrew Bain

Rob Voss

Lauren Gemmell

Lee French

Luigi Ballabio

Andy

Richard Parks

Gregory Lovell

Kev Partner

M. Mahar

Allan Kaster

Angela Penrose

Jamie DeBree

J.V. Ackermann

Geoff Palmer

A.J. Abrao

Rebecca M. Senese

J.R. Murdock

Christine Connell

Ashley Pollard

Steven Rief

John Winkelman

Steve R

Bill

Leigh Saunders

Christine

AM Scott

donald crossman

Louisa Swann

Brent Bissell

Rob Vagle

Sharon Rowse

J & M Lowry

Mark Leslie

I.G. Frederick

Rick Lohmeyer

Jeff Soesbe

Michael Kowal

James Husum

Eugenia Parrish

Teri Babcock

Debbie Nulf

Sean Roach

Ken Talley

A.R. Henle

Justin Johnson

Jennifer Brinn

John Haines

Robert McCarter

Mary Kennedy

Kate Rooney

Lana Ayers

Gerard Ackerman

Jane Reeves Newell

Werner Meyer

Stefon Mears

Travis Heermann

Ray Vukcevich

Simon Horvat

Gregory Wade Stitz
Christina York
Fred A. Aiken
Anonymous Reader
Patrick
Joshua Cooper
W.A. Brown
Damien Filer
Andrew Hatchell
James Beach
Harvey Stanbrough
Sabrina Chase
Melissa H. Taylor
Paula Whitehouse
Alexandra Brandt
Joshua Maher
Annie Reed
Ranveig Wallace
Sarah C
Felicia Fredlund
Trent Walters
J. E. Hopkins
coraa
Daphne Riordan
Gary Jonas
Chris Abela
Celine Malgen
Marcelle Dubé
Sheila Watson
Chrissy Wissler
Joanna Penn
Chong Go Sunim
Johanna Rothman

Rob Slater
Laura Ware
Danica Oakley
David Hendrickson
Angie Simon
Amy Laurens
kathryn mccloskey
Linda
Mary Fishler-Fisk
Camille Lofters
Linda Maye Adams
Katrina Tipton
Kenneth Norris
Carolyn Rowland
Mark Grant
Stuart Jaffe
John Payne
Sharon Reamer
Len Chang
Robert Battle
James Wisher
Anthony St. Clair
Lena Goldfinch
Christina Martin
Marie Laura
Kari Kilgore
Derek Miller
Keith West
Emily Williams
Michael and Nitu Gulati-Pauly
Stephen Couch
Matt Herron
David Brown

Catalyst Games
Johnny Pedersen
Tracy May Adair
Joseph Wrzos
Terry Mixon
Turner L.
Lynda Foley
Fran Friel
Lisa Satterlund
Steven H Silver
Todd Goetz
Sandra Hofsommer
Bonnie S Warford
Al Harris
R.F. Kacy
Joy Johnson
Karen Shannon
Bonnie Koenig
Michael Harbour
Lyndon Perry
Scott Tefoe
Michael Nisivoccia
Christel Adina Loar
Michael La Ronn
Ashley Pollard
Steve R
Christine
Louisa Swann
Sharon Rowse
I.G. Frederick
Michael Kowal
Teri Babcock
Ken Talley

Jennifer Brinn

Mary Kennedy

Gerard Ackerman

Stefon Mears

Simon Horvat

Fred A. Aiken

Joshua Cooper

Andrew Hatchell

Sabrina Chase

Alexandra Brandt

Ranveig Wallace

Trent Walters

Daphne Riordan

Celine Malgen

Chrissy Wissler

Johanna Rothman

Danica Oakley

Amy Laurens

Mary Fishler-Fisk

Katrina Tipton

Mark Grant

Sharon Reamer

James Wisher

Christina Martin

Derek Miller

Michael and Nitu Gulati-Pauly

David Brown

Tracy May Adair

Turner L.

Lisa Satterlund

Sandra Hofsommer